Of Walls

Sara L. Foust

Of Walls, a Novella

Published by Silver Lining Literary Services
106 Offutt Rd.
Clinton, TN 37716
www.saralfoust.com

Printed in the United States of America

ISBN 978-1-732-9047-0-5

Scripture quoted is from the King James Version of the Bible, which is in public domain.

Of Walls

Sara L. Foust

Sara L. Foust

Dear Readers,

While my recent personal mission trip to the Philippines did spark the idea for this book, please read it with your fiction-goggles on. There are strings of truth woven into this story as far as the setting, but it is a work of fiction. None of the characters are meant to secretly resemble anyone that traveled with me or that I met on my trip. And none of the events are meant to represent true-to-life occurrences. While dozing on the plane, people-watching, the idea for *Of Walls* came to me. And I told God a long time ago I'd follow where He leads. I hope you find encouragement in my newest story, my first dip into the women's fiction genre.

If you would like to read the real-life account of my mission trip, please visit: https://saralfoust.com/category/mission-trip/.

Also, I would love to connect with you. You can sign up for my newsletter to receive important updates, sneak peeks and first news alerts, and information about giveaways through my website, www.saralfoust.com.

Ezekiel 13:14 (KJV)

"So will I break down the wall that ye have daubed with untempered morter, and bring it down to the ground, so that the foundation thereof shall be discovered, and it shall fall, and ye shall be consumed in the midst thereof: and ye shall know that I am the LORD."

Chapter One

"I really need this trip."

He just looks at me. Trying to figure out my subtext? I send messages to my eyes to pretend there isn't any. I'm not brave enough to illuminate the truth. Not yet.

"Our finances are never going to get better."

I roll my eyes. Of course they aren't. There's no hope in anything, according to you. "You know, I have confidence when I get home I can take this course and provide for *myself.*"

He lifts his eyebrow.

I've crossed a line. I try to backpedal, cover my almost truths. What I want to say is, "I don't want to be married to you anymore. I'm done. I give up." My tongue hurts with permanent teeth impressions by now. If I say the things in my mind, I won't be able to stuff them back in. Won't be able to erase them. Won't be able to put the smashed bricks back into place. What if I am blatantly, brutally honest and regret it? I see the fear flitting across his eyes. The anger igniting beneath the hazel irises. "That's not what I mean." I take a deep breath. "I really need this trip."

He drops his gaze. "I know."

Does he? Does he sense the wall of barbed wire squeezing my heart? The pain? The desperation? Despair? "We will figure out the money when I get home. It's going to work out somehow. God has taken care of us this long, He won't stop now."

"I know."

Does he? Does he really believe it? Do I? My faith is dancing atop Phyllo-thin ice. I will fall into the daggers below, the icy grip of utter exhaustion and hopelessness, soon. "Thank you for letting me go."

He nods. Shoves his ear buds back into the sides of his head and directs his attention to his laptop. Conversation apparently over. Chip another layer of dough off the thin covering around my emotions. Let the chill bubble a little higher. I won't be able to breathe soon.

Is divorce ever an okay option? Besides physical abuse, can a Christian ever legitimately be divorced without God's disapproval? I rub my temples. I've thought too hard and too many times about this question. There's more confusion than clarity, and I know I'm deep into the void of the devil's tricks, but I can't stop myself. I'm so unhappy. Marriage isn't meant to be miserable.

"Mommy, I'm hungry."

I jump. How long have I been lost in thoughts, my face soaking wet? "I'm sorry, baby. I forgot your peanut butter bread." I pull her into my lap and kiss her sweet-smelling head. "Thank you for reminding me." I really need this trip. *Lord, help me be the wife and mother You want me to be.*

The front door swings open. I should turn. Should embrace him. Should be the wife I should be. I turn my back and spread the peanut butter over the hard-at-the-edges bread. We eat like poor people because our bills are so high. I chuckle mirthlessly. The animals eat well. Better than us half the time.

Adam shoves flowers in front of my nose. I fight back a sneeze, ignore the petals falling on Eleanor's bread. "Oh hon, they're beautiful." My heart buoys a little, bobs a tiny bit higher in the dark ocean. I take the bouquet of wildflowers he handpicked for me and tied with a string of grass. Redbud branches, yellow fuzzy somethings, delicate white stars. He's really listening. He's getting that I need more.

Why isn't it reaching me? My smile falls. Am I beyond persuasion?

No. I shake my head. My unbrushed curls bounce against my ears. I'm no quitter. My stubbornness has kept us together all along. Through the early years of financial hardship that have never gone away but we've learned to deal with them slightly better. Through the babies' births. Through the affair. No, I'm not a quitter.

Eleanor slips her bread from my hands, mutters a quick, "Thank you," and darts back toward the living room as Mickey Mouse blares his silly hot dog song.

Have I exhausted my supply of rubbery resilience? Of sticks-and-stones-but-words-can't-hurt-me shielding? Tears pool in the corners of my eyes again. I swipe them away, turn my face so he can't see. Maybe he will believe they are from joy. They should be. Why can't I find that particular salty reserve anymore?

I'm not strong. I'm a liar. A trickster. I should come clean. Admit to the lusts of the flesh. The loneliness. To the fact that the devil is winning the battle for my thoughts. Waging a war for the desires of my heart, the attentions of my affections. And inching his way to victory. There's an old Reba McIntyre song that sums it up awfully well right about now. But I can't remember the words. Something about a wife who married young and wonders where the rest of her life has gone?

Adam stumbles over a toy in the floor. Kicks it as hard as he can. It bounces off the wall. The apple green one I labored intensely over for hours and hours. I shrug. I can hardly notice the dent the stupid truck made. He mumbles something about things underfoot.

My heart returns to its new position. New? Old? Who can tell anymore? I guess that's my sign I need to pick up again. I'm not good enough at this whole housewife thing to keep my man happy. I would've failed Home Ec. Who am I kidding? I am failing it. Every moment of every day. No one cares that my kids are fed and dressed. He doesn't. No one cares that I've studied about each of my children's slight disabilities and agonized over therapies. Prayed endlessly for patience. Wisdom. Healing. For all of us.

I stoop and retrieve the car, scrape up an armful of dirty laundry, pinch my fingers around an empty yogurt cup, and stand erect. Black closes in the periphery of my vision. My arms are so heavy I can't feel them at all. A wave of weakness crashes from head to toe, draining the blood as it sinks into my feet. I plop onto my bottom. Hard. Catch my breath. Wait for the swirling cascade of numbness to recede. But it's okay. I've managed to hold onto everything. And not crush a child in my near-fall. And Adam didn't see. So it's okay. No one saw my weakness today. One more successful day at being superwoman with an iron external covering. And a dying internal one.

I rise, more slowly this time, deposit my items in their correct places. *Lord, don't let that happen overseas. Please.*

Maybe I should tell my doctor. What if he tries to make me stay? Better not to confess. I'm sure it's dehydration. Exhaustion. Emotional fatigue. I'll just drink more water, and I'll be fine.

"Mrs. Julie Johnson?"

The nurse calls my name, but it takes a moment to register. Yes, I'm really here. Really waiting in the foreign travels section of the health department. I rise on someone else's legs, smile somehow, and follow her through the door.

"You're going to the Philippines, huh?"

"Yes."

"Visiting family?"

"A mission trip, actually." Saying the words out loud makes it feel more real. Not quite reality, but a step closer.

"Oh."

I quirk my eyebrow. Why oh? Does she know something I don't?

"Well, I'm sure that will be great. Okay, let's get your weight."

I just love this part. Typical American stereotype that is truth.

She takes too long to balance the little weights. Just give it up already and call it one-ninety. Like she can't bear to leave the marker there. To sentence me to nearly 200 pounds. Like it matters. I'm married to a man who couldn't care less what I look like. A mother of three. No one in their right mind would think I'm attractive, so why worry?

Besides, I know what I've done to my physique over this awful, dark, depressing winter. Chocolate and carbs have been my best friends. My self-therapeutic spiral deeper and deeper into murkier waters than I've tread in years. Zoloft is a wonder drug only to a point. After so many daily calories it's probably less effective.

"Ma'am?"

"Huh?"

"I asked how tall you are."

Why does everyone ask that when the measuring thingamajig is staring at me as we speak? I don't remember, okay? Yes, I'm dumb and I can't remember how tall I am. But I can tell you which child gets which medicine and at what doses. And which lovie is their favorite. And who hates green beans but loves peas. "Um, around 5'7" I think."

She frowns but writes the number down.

Would it be very wrong to smack her? I suppose it probably would.

Nurse slim-and-beautiful deposits me in a small, bare room. "The doctor will be in here in a moment to discuss some of the issues of foreign travel."

"Thank you," I manage to squeak. What issues? I've done my research. Surely I already know the risks. I straighten my shoulders and smile as she slams the door shut. I flinch. Am

I making a huge mistake? *Lord?* His stern breath of reassurance brushes over me. No. I must go. God said, "Go," and I have to listen. There's a reason—

"Mrs. Johnson," the doctor begins addressing me before I can even see her behind the opening door. "You are going to the Philippines for a mission trip, I understand. What part exactly?"

I clear my throat. Search my memory for the strange-sounding words. "We fly into Manila first, then to Naga City, and then drive to Daet."

She doesn't bother to look at me. "Let me pull up the CDC website."

"Okay, thank you." Why am I ingratiating myself already? She hasn't done anything. I clear the phlegm lodged precariously above my lungs.

"Will you be in close proximity to farm animals?"

"Um, I don't believe so, no."

"Good. How about the jungle?"

How am I supposed to know? I'm flying to a country that I couldn't even locate on a globe six months ago. "I don't believe so."

"Okay, well it looks like we are missing some of your childhood vaccination records. Have you had an MMR vaccine?"

"Yes." I think. I'm pretty sure.

"Good. This one is essential. If you didn't have it, we can give you this today."

I rack my brain for memories. I was only five when I started kindergarten. How am I supposed to really remember? But something is telling me I did have it. "No. I just need the typhoid vaccine today, please." Put on your best smile.

"You are aware that there is a risk for these mosquito-borne illnesses as well, right?"

She hands me fliers, one at a time, with names I've never heard or seen before. What in the world is chikungunya? Dengue and Zika I think I've heard of before. My heart picks up speed, slamming into my breastbone. *You're. Crazy. Do. You. Want. To. Die. On. Foreign. Soil?*

"You'll need malaria medicine as well. And antibiotics, steroids, and sinus medicine just in case. Oh, and the malaria medicine and antibiotic, doxycycline, is known to cause secondary vaginal yeast infections. So you may want to discuss this with your primary care doctor."

More fliers enter my outstretched hand. Somehow I manage to close my fingers without dropping them to the floor.

"Okay, ready?"

I glance at her gloved hands, holding the syringe. "Mm-hmm."

"Roll up your sleeve, please."

"Oh right. Sorry."

The needle enters my skin painlessly, but when she depresses the plunger, a sharp, burning pain rushes up my bicep and deep into the shoulder socket. Is that normal? I'm too embarrassed to ask.

"You're all set. The travel bureau recommends a few things to keep in mind. Do not go anywhere alone over there. ISIS is active in parts of the country. And for up-to-the-minute information, you can sign up on this website." She hands me another flier to go with the impressive stack. "Here you will find info about terrorist attacks. Wear bug spray at all times. Do not drink any water that is not sealed. Do not eat any fresh fruit from local vendors. Wash everything you do eat very well."

She's waiting on a response from me. What am I supposed to say? My tongue is so stuck to the roof of my mouth, all I can do is smile and nod.

"I hope you have a great trip."

She does? Really? "Thank you."

"Be safe. We need to watch you for twenty minutes to make sure you don't have an adverse reaction to the vaccine. If you'll wait in the lobby, this way. Thanks."

Adverse reaction? Kind of like the way my heart is screaming in my ears? Or my hands are making the fliers look like leaves in a thunderstorm? She nudges my elbow and points to the door marked Lobby.

"Have a great day, Mrs. Johnson."

I was. Until she scared the daylights out of me and made me question my sanity. Again.

Chapter Two

Adam slams the pantry shut, opens the fridge and stands there.

I wipe my hands on my apron and force a pleasant tone. I think. "What's wrong, hon?"

"Looking for something to drink with dinner."

"I'm sorry. We're out of milk. I need to go to the store." I flash him a half-hearted grin.

"Water it is." He shuts the fridge so that my colored bottles on top rattle. How many more slams until they crash? How many until I do?

"I'll make some tea. Dinner's almost ready."

He grunts his thanks.

I lift my arm but find it is too sore. Stupid typhoid shot. There's no bruise, I checked earlier. I use my other arm to retrieve the tea bags and sugar. Is he going to ask how my appointment went? Should I mention it? If he cared, he'd ask. Right? Maybe if I get him talking about his day, he'll ask about mine. "How was work?"

"Same as usual. It stunk."

"I'm sorry, hon. I prayed for you all day."

"Thanks." Then under his breath, "Lot of good it did."

He's miserable. And I'm not helping. I should get a better job. I could work from home again. The little voice niggling the back of my mind wakes up to ask, "When would you have time?" Five in the morning, between doctor visits, midnight. I could do it. But, man, I sure don't want to.

"Kids! Dinner's ready!"

The stampede of footsteps races from bedrooms and the back porch. Chairs scrape and voices chatter in the dining room. What a blessing our full house is! Most of the time. I glance at the pantry door, mentally calculate how many more dinners I have and how many days it is until payday. *Lord, I know You say You provide every need. I trust You, but I'm worried. This trip is so expensive. Are You sure?*

I'm sure, Julie.

Tears well in my eyes as I turn my head to catch a glimpse of my babies sitting at the table, waiting for me with energy and smiles.

What if they don't miss me? Or they miss me too much and I can't get home to them?

I'm sure, Julie.

I move the kettle of boiling tea to the cool eye and take a deep breath. He's sure, Julie. You've already said you're going. Only two months. It's too late to back out.

Courage. My word for this year. Do I have enough left? Can I possibly summon from some deep, dark spring within me enough to get me on that plane?

"The car made a funny noise, Mommy!" Grace calls as she swings open the squeaky front door and races to jump on my stomach.

"Oomph." I giggle. "You're getting really big. Maybe too big to jump on my stomach like that?"

"Sorry, Mommy."

I grab her cheeks and pull her close for a kiss on the forehead. "Was it kind of this weird bumpy, stalling-out sound?"

"Mm-hmm."

"Yeah, it did that to me the other day too."

"Why didn't you tell me?" Adam's voice fills the living room.

I thought about it. But he's been so stressed lately, I just couldn't bring myself to add more to his plate. "I didn't want to worry you. I guess I figured if it broke, we'd deal with it then."

He huffs. "I'd rather know about it now." And storms into the kitchen where he proceeds to riffle through the cupboards again.

What is he looking for? I told him I need to go to the grocery. His cookies aren't in there.

"Are you okay, Mommy?"

I bite my cheek to press back the tears. "Oh, sweetie. Mommy's fine. I just need to go potty."

Grace plops onto the couch next to me, steals the remote from my hand, and flips it to the Disney channel before I can even rise from the couch.

With the bathroom door locked behind me, the tears can't be held back any longer. They gush down my face, dripping from my chin and splashing onto the floor. I press my back to the wall and slide onto my rear. Why does he have to be so cruel? Every time I do or say something, I'm wrong. I can't keep the house clean enough to suit him. I can't keep the fridge and pantry stocked well enough. Dinner was too hot. What good am I?

Snot runs from my nose, trickles down my lips. I don't bother to grab a tissue, instead swiping my shirt across my face. What difference does it make? I can feel the blotchy redness marring my cheeks, swelling my eyes, but I can't stop the torrent. *Lord, please! I'm not good enough. Why would You want me to be a missionary? What could I do to help anyone?*

I melt into a mushy puddle on the floor, curling into the fetal position and pressing my fist to my mouth. No one needs to hear my sobs. I have to be strong.

Dot wraps her skinny arms around my shoulders, pulls me close, squeezes tight. For a moment, I close my eyes and imagine everything I need is in this one embrace. It ends too soon.

"I'm so glad you're here, Julie. We've got a lot to discuss tonight. Everyone else is in the back room."

I take a steadying breath.

"You ready?"

"As I'll ever be, I suppose."

She slings her arm across me and directs me toward the private party area. "It's normal to be nervous your first trip. And you've never left the country, so it's doubly nerve-wrecking."

I nod. We enter the room, and I lock eyes with a new face. Square jaw. Buzz cut hair. Deep wells of inky-colored eyes. Is the room spinning? How about my head?

"Julie, this is Brant. He's just joined our team."

Somehow or another, I manage to shake his strong hand and not puddle onto the floor. Again. His smile penetrates something deep within me. Awakens a nerve ending buried in my stomach.

I choose the chair as far away from his outlined muscles as possible. Focus on buttering my roll and listening politely as the couple across from me regales me with tales from their last trip. My brain isn't listening. Though I try. I really try.

Lord, why this? You know I love my husband. You know my heart.

Didn't I just beg God to keep me from temptation not a week ago? I can fully recognize the attack sneaking in behind the walls, swinging in from the back, threatening every ounce of self-respect I've ever had. The devil and his minions sure know how to pounce, creep, and devour. How to niggle into the tiniest—well, maybe not so tiny right now—crack and freeze, expand, thaw, repeat until the fissure grows into a chasm. No. I will stop those thoughts in their tracks.

I love my husband.

I love my husband.

I love my—

"Hi. Julie, right?"

Where is my rearguard when I need it? I plaster a smile on my face and spin halfway to face Brant.

"How was your meal?"

"Very good. Thank you. Yours?" Why do I have that tone in my voice? I'm not some sassy southern belle. Grow up, Julie.

"Delicious. Suppose we'll have food that good over there?"

Good question. I've been so worried about leaving my children, I hadn't given it two seconds' thought. "I don't know, really."

Dot breaks in, wrapping that bird-like arm of hers around Brant's elbow. "We will eat very well. The church ladies feed us the most amazing Filipino delicacies."

Brant laughs heartily.

Great. Even his deep laugh is cute. Good grief, Julie. What's wrong with you? You're a thirty-six-year-old housewife with belly rolls and stretch marks that look like roadmaps of downtown Atlanta. Even if you were single, which you aren't, he wouldn't give you two glances if he weren't forced to be in your company for two weeks.

There, see, problem solved.

Brant lays a broad hand on my back. Innocent enough. But my heart reacts, even though I just gave it such a good talking to. "It's been great to meet you. We'll have to chat more on the plane. You have a family?"

Oh good. A safe topic. "I do." My face beams, I can tell. "Two girls and one boy."

"Good. I have a daughter. She's thirteen. What are the ages?"

His smile is so distracting, for a moment, I'm not sure. "My son is two. My daughters are eight and six." I really should mention my husband. Or his wife. "What's your wife's name?" I blurt. Smooth transition.

His grin falls a fraction of an inch. "I'm not married. Not anymore."

Oh, perfect.

I must erect another layer. Try as I might, it refuses to materialize in its normal brick and barbed wire form. Instead taking on the sensuality of water, like standing in the middle of the sea with sheer cliffs of seawater rising on either side as Moses holds his staff high. Pulsing, Ebbing. Inviting. Tempting me to feel its silky-smooth warmth.

Stop it. What is wrong with you, heart? Can't you listen to me for once?

I love my husband. I will not be weak.

"Mommy!" three choruses of little voices ring out as I swing open the front door. "You're home!"

"Hello, my babies." I stoop to scoop them into one big hug. "I missed you." My heart cringes a little. I've only been gone for three hours. How are we going to feel apart for two weeks? I've tried to imagine the pain I will feel at the separation, but I must stop myself because if I go too far down that road, I won't leave.

"Hi, hon." I pat Adam on the shoulder as I walk by his recliner. "How's it going?"

"Fine."

How was your meeting, hon? Oh, how I wish he would ask. I wait a beat. Press on despite his laser focus on the television. "We have a new team member."

"That's cool."

"He seems nice." Did I keep my voice level enough? Three little words, surely they didn't sound strange.

"That's good."

Porter runs up to me with a telltale odor emanating from his diaper-clad bottom.

"Oh, buddy. You stink."

He giggles and runs away.

"I'm hungry," Grace whines.

"I'm thirsty," Eleanor adds.

One poopy, one hungry, one thirsty, but everything's fine. I roll my eyes, take a deep breath. *He's tired, Julie. He did his best.* My self-pep talk soothes the frustration a bit.

"Well, come on, guys. Let's fix it."

What are they going to do for fourteen whole days without the gear that keeps our house turning? *Lord? Are You sure?*

I'm sure, Julie.

Watch over my babies while I'm gone. Please, Lord, protect them. Keep them safe and well fed.

I will protect all of you. I can be with you and here at home too.

I know this. I believe this. I'm still scared.

Chapter Three

Maggie rolls a few more peanut M&Ms across the space between us. I scoop them up and slip them into my lap, glancing around conspiratorially. The new manager hates snacking at our desks. She swears it shortens the lifespan of our computers. Ridiculous. Well, except that time I spilled my boiling hot black coffee on my keyboard and thought I'd have sparks. It did fry it. No sparks, though.

"Are you ready for your trip?" She pops a yellow candy in her mouth and crunches.

"I am. I think."

"I still can't believe my best friend is leaving me alone for so long. What if you catch some weird disease and have to be hospitalized and I have to keep this place going extra-long?"

I roll my eyes. "Gee thanks. I can see you are so worried about my health." Extra emphasis on the my.

"Oh come on, you know what I mean. I'm really proud of you."

"Thanks." "And then almost inaudibly, "At least someone is." My mind flashes to the discussion before I left for work this morning. He still hasn't asked for details or shown any real interest at all in my upcoming major life event. Like it isn't happening at all. I sigh. "I really am looking forward to this. I can't remember the last time I did something that wasn't revolved around Adam or the kids. I've been a mom for eight years and a wife for fifteen."

"Yeah, I know you've been down lately."

Should I pursue this line of conversation? I hate crying in front of anyone. And no doubt tears will come if I delve too deep into how I'm feeling. Whether I want them to or not. I bite my lip and throw caution to the wind. This is Maggie. She will understand, after all. "It's more than that, you know. I'm ready to do something for me. Well, not for me. For God, but by myself. If that makes sense."

"It does." She smiles and nods, urging me to continue.

"I'm looking forward to being me. To rediscovering who I am when I'm not Mom and wife and part-time desk jockey."

"You're saying you feel a little lost."

"Exactly. Don't get me wrong. I love my family and it's what I've always wanted to do, who I've always wanted to be. But I have lost sight of myself somewhere along the way. Do you think God will show me who I am again?" How to love myself and my husband again?

Maggie takes me hand and squeezes. "I'm sure of it."

I blink away the moisture clouding my eyes. "How?"

"Because I'm praying for it."

My heart warms. Maggie always knows how to make me feel better. To reassure me when I need it. Or chastise me when it's necessary. How will I fare in the Philippines all by myself with a bunch of strangers? And Brant.

I haven't told Maggie about him yet. Why, I'm not sure. But now's definitely not the time. Too many ears and noses to push their way into my business. Into my embarrassingly unfit thoughts.

"Do you think . . . He can save—?"

"I'm sure of it."

A tear trickles down my nose. I wish I was so confident. What am I going to do if God doesn't intervene and save our marriage? What if my worst fears, of having to share custody, of having to spend holidays away from my children, of having to go back to work full-time, of having to fight over the homeschooling in front of a judge, come to fruition? What if divorce is the only way for me to be happy again?

"M&M?"

Maggie slips another handful of candy into my lap, only the green ones. My favorite. *Lord, are you sure?*

I'm sure, Julie.

I kiss Eleanor's moist forehead, sandwiched in between Adam's shoulder and my body pillow. Shake Adam awake, sort of, and whisper, "I'm heading to work. My last day before the trip!"

He grunts.

When he switched to second shift at work, I thought our lives were going to be so much harder. But God used even that unwanted change to make good things happen. It freed up the morning hours for me to get a much-needed job, providing a little extra income to supplement his meager assembly line pay. And I still get to homeschool in the afternoons. We don't have to pay a babysitter. I remember these things as encouragement for myself. To add assurance that God always knows what He's doing. This is my last morning saying goodbye. "I'll see you in a couple hours." It's easy to breeze out the door this morning knowing I'm on a nearly three-week vacation starting tomorrow. Well, break anyway. The mission trip will be a lot of work, so not exactly a vacation. I shake my head. Why am I justifying my use of words to my own self?

As I drive, I tick off the mental checklist that revolves constantly in my brain. I've finalized the meal plan for while I'm gone, stocked up on all those necessary ingredients, hung a list of emergency numbers a mile long on the fridge, sorted the sensory toys and placed them in the easy-to-find cupboards, quadruple-checked the schedule and verified at least three times with the upcoming kid sitters, cleaned the house a bit, packed, gotten my shots—

Maggie knocking on the passenger window makes me jump. How long have I been sitting in the dark lot, idling? I shut off the engine, gather my purse, book, and packed lunch, and swing open the door.

"Where were you?" She smiles.

"Lost in la-la-list land." I sigh. "You remember when to come get the kids, right?"

Maggie rolls her eyes and pats my shoulder. "Relax. Everything is going to be fine. Besides, I'd say you'll miss them way more than they'll miss you."

"That's reassuring."

"You know what I mean. Beth and Morgan are really excited about our sleepover with your gang. Trust me, they will be fine."

She has a good point. And her girls do get along well with my crew. *Lord, help me miss them more than they miss me. I want them to have a blast while I'm gone.*

We step into the air conditioned lobby and catch the left elevator. It's almost always the left. Why? I have no idea. But it makes me afraid of the right one. If it's too slow to be first available, there must be something wrong with it. Right?

"Only two more days, Maggie. I don't know if I can do this." I wrap my arms around my midsection.

"Sure you can."

"There's a man."

She is so shocked, she can't speak. Which is saying a lot. Her mouth dangles dangerously open, inviting mosquitos or small birds to take nest.

"No, not like that."

The elevator dings open, but neither of us makes a move to exit.

"Like what then?"

"Going on the trip."

Her peal of laughter fills the elevator. I'm tempted to put my hands over my ears like Eleanor does when the auto-flushing toilets go off in Wal-Mart.

"Of course there's a man going. There are several, aren't there?"

I take note of her barely contained mirth. It doesn't make me feel any better. Thanks, friend, for that. "A cute one. A single one."

"And?"

"And what if I have thoughts I shouldn't have?" Kind of like I already am.

"So what? Thoughts are silent. Actions are what speak. You love Adam. I know you do. You're not going to make some crazy mistake while on a mission trip *for the Lord*."

Well, when she puts it that way. I shake my head. "Of course. Yeah, you're right."

"It's natural for a woman to notice an attractive man, Julie. Everyone does it."

I nod. That may be true. But is it natural to wonder what life would be like with him? To wonder, if I left my husband, would this new person want to take care of me? The elevator doors slide open again. We are still resting at our floor, which is slowly coming to life. People are buzzing to their desks like honey bees. I have to get off, get through one more day of work, one last day of homeschooling the kiddos, and then I will be off.

Standing atop an unstable, isolating wall, ready to leap to the other side where a new adventure awaits. A new self. A new revelation, a look at life from a different angle. I'm not ready. But in a sense I've never been more ready.

Adam is staring at me across the slick-topped Gondolier table. Clustered between our family members for my send-off dinner, he smiles. I try to return his gesture, but my stomach is upside down. Why is he suddenly so interested in my plain-old face?

"What?"

"Nothing. I'm just really going to miss you."

My smile blossoms into something genuine. How do I respond without lying? I don't think I'm going to miss him, but I can't say that. "Thank you. I'm sure you'll be fine." Not really. But with so many friends and family members helping, surely everyone will at least survive until I can get home and put things back in order.

"I don't know how you do it all, hon." He winks and takes another bite of his breadstick. "You're superwoman."

A brick, one solitary one, tumbles off the wall. "Thanks, hon. It's only ten days."

He nods and turns his attention to our son, who is trying to quietly drink the marinara. Adam grins and lets Porter slurp noisily as he drains the little porcelain dish. This is what their two weeks will be like. No vegetables unless they are pizza sauce. No bed time, either, probably. *Lord, just keep them alive until I get back. Please.*

"Three cheers for the world-traveler," my aunt Josephine calls. She lifts her cup of sweet tea my direction, and the rest of my family follows suit.

"Thanks, guys."

"Are you excited?" my niece Izzy asks. It might be the first time I've seen her come out of her cellphone all evening.

"I am. Nervous, of course. But excited."

"You know there's an active ISIS cell in the Philippines?"

My eyebrows join forces to strengthen my next words. "Oh, um, yes, I believe I heard something about that." Didn't work. They still sound weak and uninformed.

"Pretty stupid going there, don't you think?"

My gaze flicks to my sister Debbie, lost in conversation with Uncle Bert. She's oblivious to the comment her know-it-all daughter just flung across the table. Oh, how I wish I could kick Debbie in the shins under the table like when we were teenagers. I plaster a smile on my face even as my mind is whizzing. No, okay, Izzy. I had no idea there was an active ISIS cell there until the mean lady at the health department told me.

And how in the world did you find out? The lump in my throat makes it awkward when I finally reply. "I'm sure God will take care of our team."

Izzy rolls her eyes and dives back into her social media world.

Josephine signals to the waitress, who brings a sheet cake to the table, candles flickering in its buttercream icing, saving me from further discourse with my apparently more-informed sixteen-year-old niece. My face flushes as they set it in front of me and expectantly watch me squirm under their attention. Am I supposed to blow them out and make a wish? Because if so, it will be that ISIS stays on the other side of the country from me.

"Happy travels to you," they chorus. Clearly, they've had time to practice the rewritten birthday tune.

Part of me is embarrassed beyond anything I've experienced in long years. Part of me can't believe I am the reason someone's gone to so much trouble. I hope Adam had something to do with it. I'd better not ask and pop that shimmery pink bubble. I think I'll choose to believe he did and put that in the pros category. I draw a deep breath, close my eyes like I'm six, and blow gently across the cake. I wish that this trip will be a life-altering, miracle-working, me-fixing journey. And that ISIS stays hidden in whatever hole they're currently occupying. Our table erupts with clapping and someone even whistles. My cheeks burn anew. I peel my eyes open to again find Adam staring at me. What in the blue blazes is going on with him? He hasn't looked at me like that in ages. Is the reality of playing mom to three kids in my place finally sinking in? I flash him a timid smile, which he greets with a second wink. Definitely strange.

My relatives manage to limp down the home stretch and add cake to their full bellies. As they start filing out, each one stops by my chair and pats me on the shoulder, wishes me well in some fashion, and then disappears into the strangely muggy spring night. Well, except Izzy, who has subtly vanished. Maybe her phone sucked her into some alternate dimension.

Before long the kids' eyes are drooping and their full bellies urging them to rest. "Well, we'd better get going, too, Adam."

He grabs two of the kids and hustles them to the car. Wow. Helpful. I grab Eleanor's hand and lead her to her booster. As we sink into our seats up front, he takes my hand and holds it the whole way home. Wow. Sweet. My hackle feathers rise. I should be bursting with joy at his attentiveness, but there's an alarm bell sounding somewhere. Pinching. Poking. Prodding somewhere deep inside my mind. I wish it had a snooze button.

Twenty minutes later we've got three sleeping babies tucked soundly into their beds and our king size all to ourselves. No doubt Eleanor's knees will be curled into the small of my back by dawn.

"I'm taking a shower." He sends a sparkly-eyed, eyebrows-raised look my direction. "You can join me if you want."

Ah. So that's it. Should've seen it coming. Heaven forbid tonight actually be about me for once. Why is it that God made women and men so very different? Wouldn't it have been so much easier for us to either operate on a man's desires or a woman's, not separated by gulfs of different wavelengths?

I know my Biblical duties. My wifely requirements. But when did our love life turn into a chore that I'd rather skip? When did I start choosing sleep over sex? But if I don't, if I say no, he will sulk, and I will feel guilty. For days. But, hey, what do I care? I'm leaving in the morning. I chuckle. When did I develop such a mean streak?

I sigh, turn down the covers, and holler, "I'll be there in a minute." He has been so sweet all evening. And it has been a while. Longer than either of us would care to admit to a stranger. Or a friend.

Chapter Four

I can't do this.

The intercom again buzzes to life overhead. "Second call boarding American Airlines flight number 2456 for Houston, Texas. All passengers flying commercial rows ten through twenty-three may now approach the boarding gate."

My heart kicks into over-overdrive. I tighten my already burning grip on my backpack straps.

Our team pastor I met at the dinner a few weeks ago nudges me. Lewis, I think. "Where are you sitting?"

"Huh?"

He chuckles. "On the plane?"

His warm smile calms the racing. A little, anyway. I fumble for the ticket I inserted into my new neck wallet. I look like a total dork, but it does keep everything right at my fingertips. "Um, 19A. You?"

He glances at the paper in his hand. "22B."

Then who am I sitting with? Please not Brant. But surely I'm sitting with someone from our group. I literally cross my fingers as I send up a silent plea. Please not Brant.

Cool air rushes to greet me as I follow the line of boarders down the aluminum tunnel. Good ole Tennessee spring. Air conditioner needed in the afternoon. Heater in the morning. I'm glad I brought a sweater.

How long has it been since I've flown? What's thirty-six minus twelve? My brain is too anxious to switch into productive-thinking mode. Somehow my feet carry me through the plane's open door, past the smiling flight attendant with the cute bow around her neck, and into the cabin. Where are the numbers for the seats? My gaze dashes from the overhead bins to the carpet to the armrests. Why can't I find them? I'm going to look like an idiot with my lovely neck wallet dangling, my huge backpack, and sitting on some stranger's lap. Oh, there they are, neatly tucked into the little plastic lip around the air conditioner nobs. I slide into the narrower-than-I-remember-them-being seat on the single-seated side of the plane. Whew! My own personal space. No strangers to worry about. And no Brant next to me with his muscly arms.

I gaze through the oval window at the sun rising, a gentle mauve, over the Smokies. A smile creeps onto my face. I'm doing this. I'm really doing this. *Thank you, Lord, for this opportunity.* A strange sense of calm washes over me. My children will be fine. My husband will survive and miss me some in the process. The world will keep spinning. Heck, people do this all the time. Think of all the military moms who are stationed overseas for six months or more. Ten days will feel like nothing. I've survived all the other leaps of faith God has put in my path.

Brant slides past the slender man hoisting his bag into the overhead compartment. Flashes that smile of his my direction and plops into the seat across the aisle from me. Suddenly the maybe twenty-four carpeted inches separating us seems so much smaller. Oh, great. Thanks so much, Dot. I crane my neck to find her among the bobble heads appearing over seats behind me. She scooches up in her seat and grins. Gives me a thumbs-up and disappears behind the head cushion.

What am I supposed to talk about with him for four hours? I shift in my seat, turn my body slightly toward the window to my left. I risk a sideways look at him. He's resting his head on his seat back, eyes closed, soft snore escaping full lips. Good. Maybe I'll get lucky, and he'll sleep the whole way.

As the plane rumbles to life, backs from the hangar, and begins gaining speed on the runway, my smile grows. Streamers of glitter swirl in my tummy. Other side of the world, here I come.

But first, I've got to survive Houston International Airport. A city within a city. A mile-long tram, fancy ceiling decorations and lights, and full-blown restaurants. And me, with my passport in a necklace, getting ready to fly over international waters. Is this real?

Dot leads the charge, slipping between people with her all of 110-pound frame and carryon with wheels. Why didn't I think of that? I struggle to keep up, not lose sight of the group, but my stomach growls, and my attention is drawn to every savory smell wafting from the shops.

Lewis and Brant are lost in conversation, somehow carrying it on with laser-like focus amid the throngs of people. Different colored faces from all over the world, some loafing, some running. America really is quite a melting pot, isn't it?

How do I let the group know I need a potty without embarrassing myself? If I think that's embarrassing, wait until I have a midlife-lady accident. I giggle. Bad idea. Okay, think about something else. Are the kids awake yet? I glance at my watch. Probably drinking chocolate milk and watching cartoons. Hopefully, Adam is awake too. Maybe I should call and check on them?

The group pauses ahead, and I nearly slam into Brant's back. "Sorry," I mumble as I take a couple steps back.

He grins down at me. "No worries."

Oh yes, many worries. Heat flares in my chest. I'm too close. His magnetic presence is messing with my internal compass, sending the needle spinning recklessly. I back up several more steps and bump Dot with my backpack. Oh good grief. Am I the only awkward duckling in the gang?

Dot spins, grabs my elbow, and pulls me toward the restroom, tossing over her shoulder, "Bathroom break. Ten minutes until boarding starts. There." She points at the terminal across the hallway.

At the sink, Dot glances at me in the mirror. "Isn't Brant a cutie?"

Whoa, what? How exactly am I supposed to respond to that?

"If I were younger, I'd be asking that hunk of a man out on a date. Reminds me of my late Edgar when he was in his thirties."

I smile. I think.

"There's a lady at church I've been trying to set him up with for months. I think he's still a little gun-shy, you know. After the divorce. His ex-wife did a real number on him." Her voice drops to a conspiratorial whisper. "Emotionally."

I'm tempted to roll my eyes, but I'm honestly too stunned to even react. Why are we having this conversation? And why do I have this crazy compunction to ask as many questions about his past as I can? *What is wrong with me, Lord? Forgive me, please. Keep my focus on You and the work we are going to do.* "I'd better call Adam and let him know we're here."

Dot opens her mouth, closes it, as if my comment has completely derailed her train of thought.

Good. That was the idea. And to put mine back on the rails it's supposed to be on. *Lord, keep me on the right track.*

Thirty-thousand feet and six hours into our torturously long flight, I'm bored. More bored than I've been in years. And too excited to read. At first, when we boarded the behemoth flying contraption I was all stoked to have a row nearly to myself. Now I'm bouncing in my seat, itching to have a conversation with someone. I glance for the umpteenth time at the sleepy Asian gentleman to my right. He's awake! I catch his eye, smile, and open my mouth to say hi. Does he speak English?

He nods and stares at me. Waiting for me to speak instead of just staring back at him?

"Are you going home?" Was that a racial thing to jump to conclusions about?

He nods.

Whew. Why does visiting with someone of a different ethnic background make me so jittery? Maybe I should just resume staring at the agonizingly slow digital image of our plane flying over the Pacific on the screen in the seat back ahead of me.

"Are you a missionary?"

His English is surprisingly crisp. Why surprisingly? I shake my head. That self-examining thought can wait. "Yes. How did you know?"

He points to my shirt where a huge cross takes up most of my front side.

"Oh, right. Yes, there are six of us heading to the Philippines to work with a local church."

"That's nice. I pray you have much success."

He is a Christian? Geez, Julie, what's wrong with your stereotypical brain today? Change the subject. Quick. "Did you enjoy your time in the United States?"

"I did. I learned a lot."

"Were you visiting family?"

"No." He steeples his fingers in front of his chin. "My wife is very ill. I came to meet with a doctor and learn how I can help her."

"You flew 8,000 miles to meet with him in person?"

"I love her."

Those simple three words plunge a hot pin into my heart. Would Adam do the same for me? Probably not.

Would you do the same for Adam?

I cringe, mentally and physically. Would I? At this point, I don't know. I'd like to think I would. When we were

34

first married, the answer would've been an undeniable and instant yes.

"You are married?" He gestures to my ring finger, absent its band but clearly whitened from years of wearing one a little too snug.

"Oh, um, yes. I didn't want to lose my wedding ring so I left it at home."

He nods, but I can tell the idea doesn't sit well with him.

Maybe it shouldn't sit so easily with me either. I don't know. "Did you learn what you needed to?"

"Yes and no. I will travel again in a few months. If we are blessed enough to make it that far." Tears pool in the corners of his eyes.

Awe pools in the corners of mine. I want that kind of love again. To feel that pull of heartstrings, that connection. I miss it dearly. What if Adam and I can't ever feel that again? What if the resentment and the pain of the past are simply too much? What if the stress of everyday life has robbed us of something we can never recover? *Lord? What will it take for me to be happy again?*

Chapter Five

The Tokyo shore finally—finally—creeps into view. I expel a massive sigh and wiggle my swollen toes. I've never had pedal edema, not even during the pregnancies. It's miserable, I decide quickly, with the tingling sensation like ants under my skin and the ache with every tiny movement. My body doesn't seem to like fourteen-hour plane rides in compressed cabins with recirculated, dry air.

I crane my neck to peer below us. Geometrical plots of silver, looking like wet parking lots, gleam from the landscape. Trees and greenery nearby, roads winding through them. What are those? I smile at my neighbor and point.

"Rice."

Ah, of course. I guess I should have assumed, but aren't most of the rice paddies of the world in Vietnam? You learn something new every day, I guess. Especially for this sheltered country gal. Zinging ribbons of yellow course through me. On their heels, darker ones. I've never been on foreign soil before. What if I get lost? Or kidnapped? Or can't order a meal because of my blubbering southern accent? I chuckle at my list of priorities.

The plane touches down smoothly and drives for what feels like miles to the terminal. Dot rounds us up before we deplane for one last minute pep talk. Liza and her husband, James, clasp hands and hover together with nervous grins.

Brant, ever seeming to be the confident one, leans casually over a seat and smiles earnestly at me. Lewis yawns and rubs a hand down his stubbly cheek. Dot shifts from foot to foot as if she can't run from the plane quickly enough. Yet the meeting is her idea? Somehow I'm a mixture of all their emotions. Like a sponge soaking in the charge in the air.

Lord, I want to be the independent, confident woman I used to be. Capable of handling this Japanese airport and everything barreling at me from this point forward with grace and humble elegance.

Lost in my own prayer, Dot's words have been rushing by me. I catch the tail end, though, and it sticks in me like nettles. "You all watch over Julie. She's a single woman who's never traveled out of our good old country. Let's make sure we stick together."

Stick together? Yes. Watch out for poor, helpless Julie? Absolutely not.

Dot flashes a sympathetic smile my way. If I could swat it back at her with one of those electrified bug killer tennis racket thingies, I certainly would. Pointing me out like that. As if I'm some kid who needs coddling. I can feel my blood pressure rising. Bringing with it the longing to prove myself capable. It's been a long time since I've felt this way.

I kind of like it.

I've been hiding in Adam's shadow, ever the submissive wife, ever deferring to his manliness for protection, for more than a decade. It feels good to be on my own for once. To be looking out for *numero uno.* Just me and God, part of a team of adults in the eastern hemisphere of the planet. Equals. Except for in Dot's eyes, apparently.

As I turn to grab my bag I find Brant has already retrieved it for me. He holds it out, and I carefully take it, making sure our skin doesn't brush. Heaven forbid that ever happens again. I manage a thank you before I turn and roll my eyes. Thanks, Dot, for taking away the sliver of independence I've needed to regain. And thrusting a handsome knight into feeling protective over me.

I am a minority here. It's immediately obvious as we exit the tunnel. I must admit I'm a bit stunned, with my cankles and the duffel bags I feel under my eyes. The group begins mumbling about hunger, passing the groaning along like children in a game. I'm just tired. And though I've been sitting for fourteen hours, all I can dream of is sitting in one of the lounge chairs and propping my feet up for a while. Maybe dozing on the arm rest.

We are like white sprinkles on a beautiful Asian-colored cake. The people swarming around us are all so interesting and wonderfully refined. Dressed like pages out of a style magazine, with genuine smiles and a language that both intimidates and awes me. I want to kick back in the corner and watch them, learn how they tick, maybe absorb some of their fashion tips. I chuckle. I doubt at this point in the game there will be much refining of my style.

Dot and Lewis rush into the sushi bar. I wrinkle my nose and pass. "I can keep everyone's bags." I plop onto a chair and soon am surrounded by a menagerie of carry-ons and brisk thank yous. With my feet propped over top of their bags in the hopes some of the swelling will disappear before the next cabin-pressure change, I lean into the chair back and take a deep breath. What a whirlwind two days it's been!

It's breakfast time at home. Are they up yet? I punch in the numbers for my very first international call and smile as it begins to ring.

Adam's sleepy voice answers something unintelligible.

"Hey, babe. Sleeping in?"

"Mm-hmm."

"The kids awake yet?"

"Nope." He clears his throat, and I can picture him peeling open his eyelids and staring at the ceiling fan that is always on overhead. "How's Tokyo?"

"Busy. And all the people here look like they stepped out of a glamorous, 90s-something TV show."

He chuckles. "Want me to wake them?"

"No. It's all right. Just give them kisses and hugs from Mommy when they do get up. I'll try to call you again later."

"Okay. Be safe. I miss you."

My brain freezes. What am I supposed to say that isn't a lie? How can I say I don't miss him without hurting his feelings? "That bad already?"

"No. Just miss your beautiful face."

"Thanks, hon. I love you."

"Love you too."

I will miss him. I know I will. Well, I'm pretty sure, anyway. But not yet. Right now I'm still paving the way as solo momma for a bit. We haven't had enough time apart. What was the old saying? Distance makes the heart grow fonder. Something like that. There's a reason that someone coined that phrase. It took me a long time to realize it, but there's definitely truth in it. Maybe it's actually healthy for a marriage to have a few moments of individualized time. Maybe.

If Tokyo was another planet, Naga City is a different universe. My gaze remains glued to the window as we approach the airport. It's like we are flying not back in time but into another dimension. A movie world, perhaps. A documentary of long-lost tribes of the jungles of Timbuktu. Dark gray wisps of smoke float from amongst broad-leafed trees. Thatched roofs dot the openings between them, looking a part of the landscape itself. Volcanic mountain peaks rise through batting-fluff clouds. And the turquoise sea below, of whose name I'm not sure, sparkles between the islands. Ebbing, flowing, dancing around tropical beaches of white sand. Is this really real? My brain is nearly numb from exhaustion. Maybe I'm dreaming.

The plane bounces onto the less-than-new tarmac, jolting my moment of disbelief away. This is real. I'm in the Philippines. Alone. For two weeks. With mosquitoes and snakes. Foreigners who don't speak my language. And handsome Brant. Real as real can be.

The crew opens the hatch somewhere behind me. I know because a rush of hot air melts over me, like opening the oven door, bringing the acrid scent of smoke with it. There is no aluminum tunnel here. Nope, just stairs onto the scorching asphalt. I lug my bags to the shade of the open-sided airport terminal and plop them on the ground next to our group.

Dot yells over the sound of the engine on our plane taking off again, "Potty break! It's a long drive so better go now."

I glance around and realize I'm not comfortable leaving my backpack with my camera and laptop anywhere on the ground. Or out of my direct line of sight. Guess it'll have to make the trek into the unknown with me. We were warned briefly about the restrooms here. I round the corner. The ladies' room is across from the men's, like usual at home, but instead of limited visibility because of a myriad of turning walls, I can see right into the urinals. I gasp and quickly turn my head as Pastor Lewis turns his back and begins to adjust his pants. That was close. Too close.

What a way that would've been to start our trip. An intense blush heats my cheeks. But I don't have time to ponder. There's a stall empty, and I'm up. The door swings open. No toilet seat. No paper. Standing water on the floor. And the smell . . . I don't have enough hands to pinch my nose, but I sorely wish I did.

Somehow I manage to go without drenching my shorts or adding to the mess. I shouldn't be surprised at the lack of soap at the sinks, but I am. How do these people stay healthy?

Outside the airport, we find our bags are being loaded on top of a bus, Jeep-like thing. Ah, this must be the infamous Jeepneys, whose style was left behind during World War II when America took up residence for a short few years. By the look of some of them in the long line outside the airport, they may actually be 60-plus years old. Bright stickers adorn most of their windshields and shiny metal make-up. Three boys, who have to be only twelve years old, are loading our things atop a bright yellow and blue one. Seriously, I'd be shocked if they were teens yet. Is it shameful how much stuff we spoiled Americans brought? And how hard these poor kids are having to labor to make them stay in their precarious perches on the roof? Aren't they going to strap them down or something?

"Let's begin our trip to Daet with a prayer. Shall we?" Dot's singsong voice rises above the commotion of luggage banging and boys giving directions in their native Tagalog language. "James, can you do the honor?"

"Sure." He removes his cap and takes his wife Liza's hand. "Lord, we thank You for this opportunity. Help each one of us fulfill the role You've called us to. We know we each have a purpose here, show us how to honor You with our service. We ask that You deliver us safely to our final destination. Amen."

Honor Him with my service. That's exactly what I want. Not to be lost in selfish thoughts about my imperfect marriage or sinful thoughts of a handsome man that isn't mine. I am so blessed. I have nothing to long for. *Lord, help me see it. Help me feel it. Help me believe it.* I know that I can't be a vessel to minister to others as long as my thoughts are impure. *Take them from me, Lord!*

I'm in a National Geographic documentary, I think for the thousandth time. The boys that loaded our luggage are somewhere overhead. I picture them desperately hanging on to our suitcases to avoid an untimely death. In reality, they are probably lounging with their eyes closed on top of our cushiony luggage. They must do this often, as testified by their agility climbing onto the roof when we left an hour ago.

I can't believe how much smog is hanging in the air like a thick, oppressive comforter in the crowded streets. Yet in between the clusters of shanties, the clearer air hangs atop rice fields, coconut trees, and some sort of cow tied to long tethers. Birds flitter, some type of sparrow, I believe, from rooftop to rooftop, swooping in to steal grains of rice as they dry on the sidewalks near the road. Men stir the drying, yellow kernels with dark, bare feet.

There are dogs everywhere. Half-bald, scrawny, pitiful little things. They are like the birds, completely ignored. A part of the wildlife. Somehow not domesticated per se, but not seeming aggressive either. The lucky few are tied in open doorways and fed scraps, it appears.

The poverty here is more than I could have imagined. Though our windowless, seatbelt-free, bench-seat Jeepney is flying on the straightaways, when our driver slows I'm flummoxed by the lack of apparent utilities. How do these people survive? No electricity or indoor plumbing. And yet in some places, there will be a mansion sitting inside its perfectly groomed, high, brick wall. Staring down at the surrounding village, proclaiming its superiority in its high-buffeted walls and condescending glassed-in windows. Its financial prowess. Its lack of lacking for the essentials. On either side, there will be a home built from bamboo sticks and thatched, leaf roofs. A scrawny, bronzed Filipino lounging in front of it, as if there isn't enough energy left in his food-depleted body to swipe at the gnats. I'm glued to the scenery whizzing past, unable to take my eyes off it, though it boggles my mind.

As we round a corner, a horn blares, and our driver slams on his breaks. I slide into our guide and head pastor's wife from the church and quickly shift away. I am so sticky I can't bear to let her feel the sweatiness of my skin.

Mam Blessica giggles. "Filipino driving is not like America, is it?"

You could say that again. "No. Not at all." A nervous giggle finds its way from me.

Over her shoulder, through the low window made for shorter Filipino people, between two crude shacks, I spot a naked child. Squatted in the dirt, she plays with a stick, poking bugs and smiling. Such contentment and joy. She looks up, and our gazes lock. Her eyes grow wide and before I can lift my hand to wave, she disappears into the shadowed doorway to her left.

How is that she literally doesn't even have a stitch of clothing, and she seemed so happy? I have so much, and most of the time these days it's hard to find my smile. Even after four cups of coffee and a carb-loaded breakfast. With laundry mountains dotting the landscape of my morning room and a kitchen sink that never seems to be empty, with smelly diapers and cups thrown to spill on the floor, I've lost sight of the blessings that cause the chores. I have a husband who breaks his back to provide. A good-paying part-time job. And three beautiful babies who never lack for the necessities. Not really, anyway.

Where has my joy gone? Somehow it has evaporated, little by little, like a puddle after a summer storm. Leaving behind a muddy, footprint-scarred divot. Somewhere behind that heavy, sticky ugliness lies my hope. I've let it suffocate. Never giving it the time of day to surface and take a breath. Keeping it locked up tight so it wouldn't escape. Wouldn't dream and be disappointed. Wouldn't breathe and disappoint.

Wouldn't meet with anyone's disapproval.

I've kept my nose so close to the grindstone, I can't see what I'm forming anymore. Whittled away the pleasure of creating and making a life that all that is left is shiny slivers of what once was. What could have been. Taunting me with their luminescent qualities, lying on the ground to be trampled and buried under more wet mud.

I must find a way to dig it out, a careful archeologist retrieving something of such value I don't dare use large tools. It must happen with precision. With intention. And more than likely, an awful lot more brutal self-inspection.

Chapter Six

How is it that the gentlemen ended up in the air conditioned car with Blessica's husband, Pastor Joel, and the women in the stuffy, bumpy bus? Three and a half hours ago— on a two-hour trip—this backward world was the most fascinating thing I'd ever seen. But after two days of traveling, too much painful introspection, and a wall of humidity as solid as the seat beneath my tushy, I'm starting to imagine my hotel room. *Lord, please let it be air conditioned so I can sleep.*

Mam Blessica and Dot are chattering away like two squirrels bonding over a walnut, in a tin can. Laughing. How do they find the energy to do anything but keep their eyelids open?

The Jeepney slows, erasing what wind was managing to creep through the windows. A tall hotel jumps up next to us.

"Home sweet home," Dot announces cheerfully.

We made it. I could smile if I weren't so exhausted. Finally. And we didn't lose the roof boys or any of our luggage. Well, at least I don't think we did. The driver opens the rear door for us and holds out a hand to help us ladies from our metal tomb. My gaze darts to the roof, and I sigh. They are still there. "Thank you, boys."

They smile in unison. "You're welcome, *po.*"

Wait. Did I offend them by calling them boys? How old are they actually? Everyone here looks so young. Cultural differences are so scary. What if I say something wrong or out of place and don't even know it?

"Come on, Julie!" Dot calls from the doorway of the hotel. "The family camp kick-off starts in only two hours."

Will this marathon never end? My body is screaming for rest. Yet my heart is screaming for Jesus. I can't wait to meet the children at the school waiting for the white-skinned American missionaries.

Three flights of stairs with no elevator. Or air conditioning. And tiny brown lizards darting up the walls as we pass. Thank goodness the young man at the front desk offered to help me with my bags, because Brant's moment of chivalry appears to have ended. And I have no shame at the sudden disappearance of my independent streak, either. Brant hefted his bags up the stairs with no effort and bulging biceps and pectorals I shouldn't have noticed but did. And I struggled with each step just to enter the building. Ugh, I need a reset nap. Maybe then my naughty brain will be better in tune with my conscience.

I follow the front desk kid, George, down a stuffy hallway whose end is punctuated by a barred door, no glass (it's slowly dawning on me this is apparently par for the course here), beyond which wave the tops of coconut trees and blue sky. My room is at the end of the hall. My compatriots have vanished, so I have no idea where they are staying. Right now it doesn't matter one bit. They could be in a different city, as long as I have a bed I can collapse into.

As my door swings open, I'm greeted with stale air and my shoulders droop. There's no way I'll sleep well in this heat. None whatsoever.

"It's okay, *po*. Yes?"

George spins and smiles broadly. He is so kind. How can I complain about my room when he just lugged my fifty-two pound suitcases up those awful stairs? "I'm fine. Just hot."

"America is cooler, yes?"

"Yes." I nod wearily.

He enters my room, deposits my bag at the foot of my bed, and disappears around the corner. The sweetest sound enters my exhausted brain.

George pops around the tan wall and grins even bigger than before. "I turn the air conditioner on for you. All the way to ten."

I could hug this sweet boy. Never have I been more excited about such a basic luxury. "Thank you so much."

"*Salamat, po.*"

I wrinkle my brow.

"That means thank you in Tagalog. With *po* being a sign of respect."

"*Salamat, po.*" I'm sure my accent is horrible, and I can't quite mimic his syllable stresses, but his chest swells nonetheless. He has taught me my first Filipino word.

George slips silently from the room, and I slip my tennis shoes from my swollen, hot feet and collapse onto the bed, relishing the feeling of the cool air blowing across my body. My eyes slide closed as my forehead begins to feel tacky. The last twenty-four hours have been so insane. So far outside my comfort zone. Did I really leave my children and husband and fly across the world?

Moments later a knock at my door makes me jump. My heart kicks into overdrive, pounding my lungs awake. I didn't mean to sleep! What time is it? Another knock spurs me to motion. "Just a minute." I stumble to the door, peek through the peephole, and gasp. Brant.

I open the door a crack and smile. "Yes?"

"You okay? We were supposed to meet downstairs five minutes ago. They are threatening to leave you." He places a broad hand on the door near my head and lowers his voice. "I wouldn't let them do that, of course."

Words. I need to speak words. Somehow my tongue feels tied in knots along with my insides. "Th-anks."

I'm drawn to his eyes. Pulled by them to places I can't go.

He chuckles. "Are you ready?"

"What? Oh yes." I slip through the doorway and start down the hall.

"Aren't you forgetting something?"

I stop in my tracks. My unusually hard, slick tracks. My shoes. What a total dork I am! As I turn, I bow my head to hide the intense blush burning my face and neck. Slip under his arm still holding my door for me and catch a whiff of soap and spicy Gillette. For a very brief moment, I savor the clean scent. But then I shake my head, grab my shoes, and force my stupid clown feet into them. My backpack feels so much better without the extra toiletries and medicines stuffed into it. I swing it to my shoulders and rush to the door. Why am I acting this way? It's completely inappropriate. Who knew the devil would follow me to the Philippines? I thought the fight would be over once I forced myself onto the plane and showed him that I wasn't turning back. I was wrong.

Brant hasn't budged. Still roguishly handsome and smiling and tempting. Ugh. I'm tempted to slap myself in the forehead. Maybe it would reset the jammed gears since the nap didn't seem to. Maybe it would help to remind every cell that I'm. A. Married. Woman. Maybe not happily at the moment. But married nonetheless. And I know by heart that even lustful thoughts are adulterous and sinful. *Lord, help me out here!*

Brant's footsteps fall heavily in behind me. Would he notice if I ran down the stairs? I roll my eyes at my own thoughts and am so grateful when the lobby arrives sooner than I felt it would. Dot looks at me and taps her watch, frustration evident in her frown.

"Sorry, I fell asleep." Surely I wasn't the only one. But I guess maybe they remembered to set their alarms. Like normal, rational adults. The group moves as one, like a school of those flashy, silver-sided fish on Finding Nemo, through the door. Even Brant. George flashes a sympathetic smile. I groan and hurry to catch up. At least they didn't see me shoeless and flustered a moment ago. Every minute of this trip has been different than I hoped. Leave it to clumsy, confused, scared Julie to make a fool of herself.

Squeezing into a cramped metal sidecar in a skirt with a giant backpack alongside Liza wasn't exactly what I pictured. At least she let me sit on the outside, away from the heat of the motorcycle attached to us with its own little metal frame. James's long legs are dangling precariously far over the motorcycle's rear rack. Does that not make him nervous? Does it not make Liza?

Talking would be nearly impossible, the sound of the muffler buzzing in our ears the way it is. Are all of these little metal pods this loud? Or is this one missing a piece?

The trip to the schoolyard flies by. Most literally. I giggle. Oh, if only Adam were here to appreciate my silly puns.

Whoa. Did I really just wish for my husband's presence? When was the last time that happened? This is a good thing. I nod vigorously. A very good thing.

"You okay?" Liza yells close to my ear.

"Oh, um, yeah. I'm fine." Just a nut you're riding in the trike with. Who has conversations with herself. And celebrates little thoughts that would mean nothing to others. But, it is a big deal. Isn't it? I want Adam. Even for just a moment. That's a good start. I hope.

We slow down for foot traffic ahead. Downtown Daet is like nothing I've seen. People are milling everywhere, jogging across the street, dashing in front of vehicles that just somehow know when to stop before they kill a pedestrian. Dogs, like walking vegetation that is unimportant and a natural part of the landscape, are scattered everywhere but completely ignored. Vendors are packed along the sidewalks, bins of fruit, vegetables, grains, and leaves of all sorts color the scene. Behind these, storefronts of plain block and wood rise. Dirty, dusty-looking buildings, their doorways filled with smiling women and children. Wide-eyed toddlers stare at us right along with their parents. Are we celebrities or terrorists in their eyes? I certainly hope the former.

"I fell asleep too." Liza ducks her chin and smiles sheepishly. "If it weren't for James, I would've overslept."

The honey-sweet warmth of her words washes over me.
"Thank you. That was a bit embarrassing." Only a bit? Ha!

"No need. I'm sure we will all see sides of each other
we hadn't expected here."

"I hadn't thought of it that way."

"I am sure at home you are the most organized, in-
charge mom we could imagine."

I lift my head a fraction higher. "Thanks. I try. It's not
always easy managing a household with three young ones."

"I imagine not. I only have two teenagers to keep going,
and it's exhausting. It sure is hot."

The trike hasn't moved in at least two minutes. "Yes, it
is. I mean, I knew it was a tropical island and all, but I never
could've imagined." To hammer in my point, I peel my sticky
shirt away from my stomach a bit. "I was dry when I left the
room."

Our loud laughter gets James's attention. "What are
you two lovely ladies having such a good time about?"

Liza pats his knee through the sidecar window.
"Nothing, dear."

He encloses her hand with his own. "I love to hear that
beautiful laugh of yours."

I nudge Liza in the side. "How sweet."

"Yeah, I got me a good one."

I wish I did. I wince. Did I really just think that? It's not
fair. Adam works so hard to provide for our family. He is sweet
when he isn't exhausted. Shame on me!

The motorcycle finally pulls away, turns right, and zips
down a narrow alleyway. How long have Liza and James been
married? They are so gentle and sweet to each other. I do wish
I had that. I press my lips together and nod. Maybe I will again.

I lean back and take a deep breath. Calmness ebbing
over me. *This trip is about so much more than me teaching the little ones
here, isn't it, Lord?*

Chapter Seven

The school yard where we will spend the next several days working with families and having church is not exactly what I pictured. Not really better or worse. Just different. There is a long, low concrete building sitting at the back of the area. Colorful doors stand open to what I presume are the classrooms. The walls have been painted white and decorated with a menagerie of flowers, birds, and trees. It's rather beautiful. A grassy yard boasts a concrete slide and a volleyball net. The only playground equipment to be spoken of. To the left is a large covered pavilion of sorts where plastic chairs are lined out like an assembly. All of this is surrounded by a concrete wall higher than my head. To keep kids in? Or dangers out? Mango trees sparsely dot the landscape where tiny sparrows flitter among their leaves.

As we stroll toward the pavilion, beautiful faces of all ages smile at us from the nooks and crannies. Too shy to approach us? A group of school-aged children runs to greet us, darting away again as quickly as they came. Dot leads us to a registration table where young ladies are handing out name badges. Both of the girls seated behind the table look at me and begin to giggle. My heart warms and lights up my face with a smile. "Hello."

Their giggles intensify, but they do not speak. Are they laughing at the sweaty American or is something else happening that I'm not getting? The rest of our group wanders toward a garden area filled with flowers and shade, leaving Liza and me to fend for ourselves at the table.

"Why are they laughing?" I whisper.

Liza looks at me with the same embarrassment I'm feeling reflecting in her eyes. "I don't know."

Do I have a booger in my nose or something? The giggling girls have multiplied and now I'm virtually surrounded by them. One nudges another in the side, mumbling something that is definitely not the one word George taught me. Finally one who seems a bit older than the others steps forward.

"Welcome to our school. We are glad we, I mean you, are here." She blushes and retreats to the safety of her giggling friends, who have renewed their nervous laughter. "I'm sorry. My English is not so good."

Ah. So that's it. They are afraid to speak and embarrass themselves in front of us. "Oh, I thought you did very well." I smile broadly. How humbling! Why should they be nervous? Don't they realize I'm the one who is scared out of my sweaty socks?

Suddenly everyone is speaking at once, touching my shoulders and pointing to my ponytail and admiring my skin. "So beautiful," they are saying even as I shake my head.

No. I'm not beautiful. Not at all. I'm a mom with stretch marks and a waistline bigger than I'd like. Split ends and swollen feet. Eyebrows that haven't been waxed in years and sweaty armpits. And socks. How can they croon about me? "Thank you, girls. But, truly, you are the ones who are lovely."

This brings an unintelligible wave of murmuring and blushing. I spot Liza a short distance away surrounded by a similar group of girls. Dot and the men are seated in the pavilion, visiting with Blessica and Pastor Joel.

How can this be real, Lord? There's nothing special about me, yet these girls have already made me feel welcomed and adored. I don't deserve that. I'm here for them, not the other way around.

"Come on, *Mam* Julie. It's starting."

I allow them to chauffeur me along, like I'm being carried in a current of walking wildflowers, each of them vying for a position at my side. The girls usher me to a seat near Liza, who is waiting out of breath and flustered. I grin at her, take my seat, and wave to the retreating girls. "That was something, wasn't it? I feel like a celebrity."

"Me too," she whispers. "It's weird."

"Kind of fun, though. Did you hear the boys whispering about the men being giants?" I clap a hand to my mouth to hide a seriously loud laugh.

Liza's top lip disappears behind the bottom one as tears of laughter sparkle in the corners of her eyes. "It made James so uncomfortable." A snort escapes her smile.

"I know!"

Pastor takes the stage and picks up a mic. I press a finger to my lips and try desperately to stop the fit of giggles about to overtake me. I'm as bad as the youngsters with their nonstop chuckling.

"We are so glad to have our friends from America with us for this fourth annual family camp," Pastor says as he smiles down at us. "Please give them a warm welcome."

The crowd applauds. I want to turn to look at them, but I feel so out of place.

Pastor Joel beckons us with excitement. "Please, American Team, come to the stage."

Wait. What? We just got here and already they want me to speak? I wasn't supposed to teach until tomorrow, and then only children. My heart begins to pound an outrageous rhythm. I can't get up on this stage in front of all these people and *talk*. What would I say that they would understand? *Lord, please help me know what to say. Only words You want me to speak.*

I rise on robotic legs and follow the rest of our team, up the steps, onto the stage. And stare into their beautiful, upturned, expectant faces.

Pastor Lewis begins, "I am honored to be here. Thank you for your hospitality and for making us already feel so welcomed. I am excited about this week." He passes the microphone to Dot.

She smiles broadly as she takes it. "It is so good to see you all again. How I've missed you this last year. My, how you little ones have grown! I'm thankful to be with you, and I can't wait to get started."

James takes the mic next and grabs Liza's hand tightly. "My wife and I have saved a long time to be with you. And because of God's wonderful blessings and grace, we finally made it. It is a privilege to be here."

Liza shakes her head when James offers the microphone and passes it straight to Brant. "Well, I'm not much on speaking in front of crowds. I'll just say thank you for having me."

Somehow it is my turn. The last few minutes feel like mere seconds. Not nearly enough time to be ready for this. I hate public speaking.

But you love Me.

Yes, I do, Lord. I take a deep breath. Words come from my mouth, my voice sounding strange in my ears. "Thank you for your smiles. I feel very blessed to be here."

Amens float calmly around me.

"I know God has big plans for all of us."

I hand the microphone back to Pastor Joel. I did it. I survived those ten seconds. And it wasn't nearly as bad as I thought it might be. My shoulders straighten a bit as I retake my seat.

The bits of sky I can see beyond the roof of the pavilion and through the trees are lighting up with the last of the day's sunlight. Reds and oranges dancing on pillowy clouds. It's too early for sunset, yet this day has been so long, it feels right.

The kick-off ceremony begins with several songs I am not familiar with, but I try to stagger along the best I can. Soon Pastor Joel is welcoming Lewis to the stage for the message. I can feel every fiber of my body sinking in exhaustion. Like my muscles and bones are shrinking and I am becoming more a part of the chair than a human being. If it continues, I'll be a puddle on the concrete floor before long. A steaming, sticky pile of mush. With full darkness comes a tiredness I've never felt. Not even after giving birth and being up at all hours of the night.

When was the last time I had to pee? I groan inwardly. When was the last time I drank any water? Though I've sweated probably a gallon, I haven't. Not since the plane. What an idiot I am! I'm in a tropical country, and I've let myself get dehydrated on the first day.

As if I said the thoughts aloud, a young man brings a cooler, squats at the end of our row, and passes delightfully cold, sweating-with-cool-condensation bottles of water. I twist off the cap and tilt the wonderful liquid to my lips. And drain the entire bottle in moments.

Pastor Joel welcomes Lewis to the stage with a long, flowery speech. I find myself drifting off, whether I want to or not. My brain is simply too exhausted to pay attention to the details. A large bat swoops into the mango tree next to the pavilion, grabbing my attention and piquing my interest. Did anyone else notice him? It doesn't seem like it. I've never seen a fruit bat in person. How cool! Why am I the only one who notices these things? Is there something wrong with me?

It seems like it's rather always been that way, though. I spot hawks on power lines when Adam couldn't care less. Deer grazing at the fringes of lush fields. Blue-tailed skinks climbing the boards of our porch rails. Lightning bugs flashing on the walls of our bedroom.

I force my attention back to Lewis up on the concrete stage. A tiny brown lizard is dancing on the wall behind him, tongue flicking for bugs I can't see. Tamping down a giggle, I shift in my seat and mentally chastise myself. What is wrong with me? We are in church, for Pete's sake.

Focus.

I wish there was more water in my empty bottle. Maybe that would help my thought train.

"Why are you here?" Lewis begins. "There could be a lot of different reasons. Have you asked yourself that question yet? Really probed deep for the answer?"

I don't know. Have I?

"Maybe you're here because you want to teach your children about Jesus." He pauses to give the parents a chance to nod and murmur yes. "Maybe you're here because you're a pastor of one of these wonderful missionary churches." Men on the front two rows say amen. "Maybe you're here because there wasn't anything else to do in your sleepy little village on a weekday evening." People chuckle. "But have you asked yourself, 'What am *I* really doing here?' "

Yes. I am here to serve. Scratch that. To humbly serve. That's a noble reason, right? A satisfactory answer?

Lewis points right at me. "Why are you here, Julie?"

My heart stops dead in my chest. Does he really want me to answer or is he just making a point? I part my lips but all that comes out is a whispered, "Ummm."

"Why are you here, Pastor?"

I expel the breath I was apparently holding as Lewis moves on to his next target. Thank goodness, he didn't expect an actual, out loud answer from me. I've already used up all my bravery at the mic a few minutes ago.

Lewis smiles. "We should all be here for one reason and one reason only." He pauses for a long moment. "To see souls saved for Jesus." Again, he pauses and lets this settle over the now silent crowd. "I'm not trying to hurt feelings, but if you are here for another reason, you need to pray. Matthew 28:19 says, 'Go ye therefore, and teach all nations, baptizing them in the name of the Father, and of the Son, and of the Holy Ghost.' Yes, it is good to teach our children. Yes, it is good to support our church. Yes, it is good to serve Him. But our main task, our main calling is to *lead souls to Jesus*. That must be our primary focus. Our number one goal.

"Is it yours?"

Lewis is speaking directly to me, though he isn't looking at me. No, God is. He sent this message for me and me alone. Why am I here? Is it truly selfless? I shake my head and don't care who sees the tears beginning to pool in the corners of my eyes.

Lord, I'm so sorry. Yes, I want to see souls saved, but I confess I have thought of other reasons for being here. I've even thought a time or two maybe You sent me to prepare me for divorce. I know better. Forgive me. Help me surrender my will to Your will. Help me hone my spiritual focus. I swipe at the tears streaming down my cheeks, but Lewis's next words have escaped me. I glance around and realize I missed something important. Inside, though, the importance has already been understood. I can feel the tough exterior walls around my heart shaking loose. Cracking at their foundations. *Lord, please! I want to see these babies sitting around me saved! Nothing else matters.*

The rest of the preaching is a blur. I've been handed a metaphorical microscope, and it is shining clarity onto my heart. Like a burning beam of sunshine directed through the lens, purging me, shaping me by fire. It isn't comfortable, but I know it is necessary.

"Won't you come to Him tonight?" Lewis pleads.

Chairs scrape against concrete all around me as groups of children rush to the altar. I've never seen anything like it. In a matter of seconds, the altar, the stage, and the aisle between me and the stage are filled with kneeling children of all ages. *Praise You, Lord!*

My heart beats harder in my chest and though my easily-embarrassed, I-can't-go-pray-I'm-the-missionary mind wants me to keep my seat, I shove aside the self-consciousness and dive in next to a group of teen girls. Releasing what is left of the tears and burden I've been carrying, I sob along with them. *Lord, forgive me. Forgive me!* My weight lifts, and suddenly I feel an overwhelming need to pray for the girl to my right. I have no idea what her name is. No idea if she understands English or is lost or saved or anything about her. It doesn't matter. *Lord, I beg You, knock on her heart. Speak to her in the language only You can utter. It is universal. It is understandable by every heart. Save her soul, Lord. Now, please. In this very moment.*

My prayer is interrupted by a light tapping on my arm. I raise my eyes and am met by the deep, chocolate-brown ones of the girl next to me. Something passes between us that needs no words. She has accepted Jesus. She lunges for me and wraps her arms around my neck, squeezing briefly and dropping her arms as redness climbs up her face.

"*Salamat, po,*" I whisper as I pat her folded hands.

She beams a wonderful, missing-toothed smile at me, pure joy encompassing her features, and radiating onto me. A peace I've not known in a long time fills me. Though I am exhausted physically and mentally, my spiritual body wishes this service could last all night.

Chapter Eight

I can't remember the last time I took a cold shower. Even at home, on the hottest summer day, after the hardest yard work, lukewarm was as far right as I was willing to push the lever. Though the ice cold water raises gooseflesh on my arms, I am loathe to turn it up. Tomorrow morning, bright and early, we will be in the middle of another scorching Philippine day. No breeze. Air so sticky my clothes are soaked before I make it to the curb. A cold shower and my air conditioned room, such bliss in the middle of my body's struggle. The local peoples do not have such amenities. Should I feel guilty?

The shower in the room next to me is running too. Brant's room. Paper thin walls allow me to eavesdrop on his habits but not quite his words. I place my hand on the cool tile separating the bathrooms. He is just on the other side. Naked and . . .

Stop it, Julie. That is not anywhere your thoughts should be. Lord, there's definitely something wrong with me.

I shut the water off and get dressed hastily. Check my cell phone for the hundredth time. Finally! It is 10:00 PM and I can call home.

Adam picks up on the fourth ring, grogginess lacing his hello.

"Hi, hon. How's it going?"

"Good. We slept in."

Again? "You're just now getting up?" The littles never sleep this late. Has Porter been in his room crying for me all morning, and Adam didn't hear him?

"Yeah, we stayed up late."

Of course they did. When Daddy's home, the rules fly out the window. I chuckle. Good. They should be having fun. "I miss you guys."

"We miss you too."

"Be honest with me, are the kids okay? Are they missing me much?"

Adam hollers at Grace to come to the phone. "They haven't been bad, hon. Really. We are just fine without you."

Just fine? Just fine. A blade of ice slices into my mommy heart. I want them to be okay. But just fine without me? Does that mean they don't need me at all? If I died over here, would they even miss me? Sudden tears claim my eyes.

"Hi, Mommy."

Grace's voice makes the accumulated tears fall, trickling down my cheeks at a rapid pace. "Hi, baby," I manage to choke out. "Mommy misses you so much."

"I miss you too, Mommy. Nana is coming to take us to McDonald's today!"

"Oh, that sounds like fun!" I swipe at my running nose. "I love you, baby girl."

"Love you too. Here's Porter."

I can hear her laughter retreating from the phone as she runs to play. "Hi, Momma."

"Oh, hi, buddy. How are you doing?"

"Hi, Mommy!"

I chuckle. His phone skills haven't quite developed yet. "I miss you so much."

Porter's voice drops to a whisper. "Yeah."

"I love you."

"Love you."

There is a long pause, and then Eleanor's voice rings through. "Hi, Mommy!"

"Hi, baby doll. What are you doing?"

"Playin'."

"Are you having fun?"

"Yes. We going to McDonald's today wiff Nana."

"I heard that. Sounds like so much fun. I miss you, munchkin."

"Miss you too, Mommy. When you coming home?"

"Eight more days."

"Okay."

Eight whole days. Am I really going to be gone that long? How will I manage? With this hole in my heart, where my babies should be, growing larger each moment. I need to hold them. To hug them and tell them I love them and kiss their soft cheeks. "I love you, Ellie."

"Love you too, Mommy. Bye!"

"No, wait." But it's too late. She's run off to play. And I'm happy she's happy. But I wasn't ready to lose their tiny voices yet. *Lord, I'm not going to make it.*

But I'm stuck. It's not like I'm just a few hours away, able to get in my car and drive home. No. I'm 8,538.3 miles away in a country I don't know anything about. I would probably get kidnapped before Naga. Ransomed for a meager penance. Or stuck in Manila with no clue how to make it to the airport.

"Hey, babe."

I hiccup, "Hey."

"You okay?"

"I just miss you guys. This is really hard."

"It's okay, Julie. Remember why you're there?"

"Mm-hmm."

"God has a plan. And we are fine. Get some sleep, okay?"

"'Kay. Love you."

"Love you too."

I hang up just before the sobs I've been holding back break through. My throat aches with the intensity. "Lord, please. I miss my babies so much it physically hurts. Help me!" My mind flashes to Liza. "Lord, if I'm meant to receive comfort from someone, please put it on her heart to come to my room."

A knock on the door makes me nearly jump out of my skin. Okay, I prayed for it, but I didn't really expect it. I wipe my face on my shirttail and whisper, "Thank you, Lord."

"Julie, are you okay?"

No. My heart drops to my toes. It's not Liza's but Brant's voice echoing through my door. What do I do? "Um, yeah, I'm fine." With my hand on the door handle, I lean against it and press my forehead to the fire escape sign decorating its room side.

"I thought I . . . um, okay. Just checking."

Those arms, those wonderfully strong, warm arms could wrap around my shoulders and hold me. Could comfort me very well, I'd bet. And I wouldn't be alone. I twist the handle a fraction of an inch.

No, Julie.

Is it my conscience or the voice of God in my heart? Either way, it's right. "Thanks for checking on me, Brant. I'm fine. Just exhausted and going to bed. Good night."

"Night."

His footsteps retreat; his door clicks shut. I sigh. That was too close. *Lord, help me long for my husband.* I'm not quite there yet, but I want to miss him. That's progress, right?

I collapse onto the bed, the endorphins from my cry fest relaxing all the muscles in my body. The mattress is comfortable, the covers fluffy and clean, and the cool air blowing onto my face heavenly. I picture Grace, Eleanor, and Porter's faces as I slip into the blackness of much-needed sleep.

Chapter Nine

The morning sun points a beam directly for my eyelids through the partially opened curtain on the balcony door. How do the people of the Philippines wake at 5:00 AM? Why does the sun rise so very early here?

My room is so cold, I can't imagine climbing out from under my covers in my jammies. Can't I just stay cocooned in the warmth of this wonderful comforter a little longer? A smile slowly spreads over my face. I meet my class today. The precious preschoolers I haven't even spoken to but know I will love. God has work for me to do.

I throw off my covers, grab the photo of my family, and plant a kiss on its laminated surface. "I love you guys."

My Bible beckons to me. When was the last time I had such peace and quiet for my prayer time?

Galatians 5:24. "And they that are Christ's have crucified the flesh with the affections and lusts."

Oh, Lord, You gave me a whopper this morning, didn't You? I can't help but chuckle at God's timing sometimes. *I am far from perfect, Lord. Help me put aside fleshly desires today, selfish desires, and to help these children.*

I'm reminded of the conversation where I told my babies before I left that I would miss them so much and that the mommy in me didn't want to leave. But that I thought the children of the Philippines deserved to have someone teach them about Jesus too. They smiled and said okay. But imagining what was coming and doing it are two totally different things, I'm learning. I feel so small. So unworthy.

Help me be a light to the precious babies I'm going to meet today, Lord. Help us break down language and cultural barriers and get Your word across to them.

It's going to be a great day. I feel it in my bubbly heart.

The air in the lobby is surprisingly crisp. I glance at my phone again. Where is everyone? Didn't we say 6:00 AM? It's only five after.

A light tap on my shoulder makes me jump. I spin and meet the sheepish grin George is giving me with a hesitant one of my own.

"They've already left, *Mam.*"

"What?"

"I didn't mean to eavesdrop, but they said you were late again. The tall gentleman with all the," he points to his upper arm and lifts his eyebrows.

"Muscles?"

"Ah, yes, muscles. He told them he thought you might not be feeling well, and so they decided to head for the church and not disturb you."

"He what?" How dare he! Angry tears spring to my eyes. I shove them aside as fear quickly threatens to replace them. I have no idea how to get to the school yard on my own. And, even if I did, would it be safe?

My feet carry me of their own accord on a pacing line along the entryway.

"Shall I telephone a cab for you, *Mam*?"

What do I do, Lord?

Boy, the devil never rests, does he? How could Dot just listen to Brant and not even bother to check with me?

"*Mam?*" George is staring at me, waiting for a grown-up, confident answer.

"Yes. Yes, please. Do you know the address of the school?"

"Which one exactly, *Mam*?"

My pulse startles and begins to pound. I look like a fool! Think, woman. "Um. I'm not sure."

"I saw *Mam* Blessica this morning. Are you with her church?"

"Yes!" Too much enthusiasm there. "I mean, yes, we are missionaries working with their church at the school."

His smile relieves much of the tension. "Come with me, I think a trike will be the fastest way."

I follow him through the door and past the flowery courtyard to the curb. He flags down a silver trike with a young man in a tee shirt driving.

"Please take her to Daet Elementary School."

The driver nods.

I squeeze into the side car and sigh. "Thank you, George. Really."

As the driver zips into traffic, passing on the shoulder, I lean back into the seat. Everything's going to be fine. I can do this.

Rice fields and coconut trees rush past. The same huge bulls that look more like water buffalo staggered on long ropes by the rings in their noses stare at the traffic passing nonchalantly. Barefoot men smooth parcels of harvested rice on the sidewalks, drying the yellow grains in the sun.

I can feel the adrenaline fading and my body relaxing. It's such a beautiful country. Poor yet humble. Meager yet bountiful. As we cover more miles, the houses stretch farther apart.

Why is it taking so long to get there?

The drive to the hotel last night wasn't more than ten minutes. Was it?

Why doesn't anything look familiar?

Oh, my gosh. I am alone, in a trike, in a third-world country, with a stranger who doesn't speak English. I have no idea where I am. And, I discover as I pull my phone from my pocket, I have no cell service.

I'm going to die.

My innocent-looking motorcyclist is kidnapping me, and I'm never going to see my family again. My heart pummels my ribcage. All the lessons my daddy taught me over the years come screaming back. *Be aware of your surroundings. Don't get in strange vehicles alone. Always know where you are and where you are going. Have a backup plan.*

I have done none of them, and now I'm going to be another statistic on the nighttime news. I wring my hands. *Lord? Surely this isn't Your plan for me.*

The motorcycle slows down. Could I survive if I flung myself out? Could I even fling myself out? My luck, my giant hind end would get wedged in the opening, and I'd be dragged to my death. Or at least make a giant fool of myself.

Over the whine of the motorcycle engine, the sound of children laughing reaches me. What? Surely if the driver were planning to kill me, there wouldn't be an audience of kids. He pulls onto the shoulder, smiles through the small window, and gestures somewhere to his left that I cannot see.

On shaking legs, I wiggle free and stand erect. There, across the traffic, sits the school. Exactly as I remember it from the night prior. Filled to overflowing with children of all ages. I am such a dork.

The driver is smiling at me, staring at me, in fact. What is he doing? He lifts an eyebrow and nods at my backpack.

I could smack myself. Duh, I have to pay him. "How much?"

"Fifty pesos."

That seems a little steep, but who am I to argue? He has saved my life this morning. The one that wasn't ever in any danger, apparently. But, for some reason, I still feel indebted. I hand him a hundred pesos and nod my thanks.

Crossing the road, I feel like the frog on the old Atari game. Dot runs to meet me at the stone archway entering the school yard.

"I'm so glad you're feeling better, Julie. Come meet the children."

Feeling better, eh? I bite my tongue. Now is not the time nor is it the place. So I just nod and smile. I can tell Brant just how thankful I am for his looking out for me later.

"Children," Dot says, "meet *Mam* Julie. She is feeling much better now and will be able to teach you today."

The little ones turn their expectant faces toward me, and my heart melts. The anger I felt five steps ago evaporates. None of them speak to me, but hopefully by tomorrow we will be more comfortable with each other.

"This is Anna. She is your helper and interpreter." Dot slips out the door, leaving me with a blushing, silent woman who looks like she might be seventeen.

The classroom boasts a concrete floor, several wooden desks, and a chalkboard that has seen brighter days. But colorful touches add a sense of peace and hope to the room. Bright curtains fluttering in the slight breeze, a painted flower on the block wall, children's drawings hanging on the far board. Its humbleness is its beauty.

Suddenly, I'm nervous, with clammy hands and dry mouth and everything. These precious babies are waiting on words of wisdom, and I've lost my train of thought.

Anna smiles at me. "Would you like me to tell them anything?"

"Um, yes. Tell them I am so happy to be here and that I'm sorry I am late."

Anna interprets for me, using her hands in big motions to communicate my sentiments. Too soon the spotlight is once again on me. That seems to be happening a lot here. These kids are just like yours. They like candy and laughs. And apparently animated speeches. I take a deep breath, exhale slowly. You can do this. "I got lost this morning. I was so scared!" I make a scared face, acting like I'm chewing on my nails. Their spontaneous laughter is music to my ears.

"I prayed so hard." I fold my hands and bow my head. "And I looked at my driver." I widen my eyes and make another funny face. My efforts are rewarded with more giggles. Even Anna is smiling. "But God brought me here to see you. And I am so very glad to meet all of you."

Sitting on the floor, with my legs folded under me, I wish I could grab them up in a big hug. "You know what?"

One girl who is particularly thin whispers, "What?"

"God protected me. He loves me, just like He loves you." I retrieve my Bible from my backpack and open it to Matthew. "Did you know Jesus has a special love for children?" Many of them nod, but a few shake their heads. "Well, He does. Let me tell you a story about a time when Jesus made a point of calling children to Him."

The more open air outside the classroom feels wonderful on my sweaty brow. I screw open the lid on my bottle and take a long sip of tepid water. Pastor Lewis is stretched out on a concrete bench under the gazebo near the kitchen. I cast a glance around. No sight of Brant. Good. I glide to the pavilion, feeling lighter than I have in a while. Teaching the children was why I came. It feels good having the first lesson under my belt.

"How was your morning class, Lewis?"

"Wonderful. And yours?"

"They are so precious." I smile at the kids chasing a blow-up beach ball across the courtyard. Such joy in simple things. "We Americans are awfully spoiled, aren't we?"

He groans as he sits upright. "I miss my air conditioned classrooms at my million dollar church." He waggles his eyebrows and grins.

I laugh.

"Yes. We are spoiled absolutely rotten." His tone grows more serious. "Are you okay?"

How much should I share with him? I don't want to make Brant look bad. But I want to be honest too. "I'm fine. I'm not sure why Brant thought I needed to stay behind."

Lewis frowns. "I should have checked on you."

"It's not your fault." Flames spike in my chest. I lower my voice. "I was really scared. I thought I was lost and being kidnapped."

He chuckles. "I'm sorry, Julie. It won't happen again, I promise you."

"Thank you."

Brant's tall frame appears from around the corner. "Mind if I join you?"

I resist the urge to roll my eyes. "Excuse us, will you, Pastor Lewis?"

He smiles knowingly. "Of course. But remember what the Bible says, 'Be ye angry and sin not.'"

"I'll do my best."

Lewis slips past Brant, who slides into the spot catty-corner to me. His knees brush mine, and for a moment a spark begins to flare in my stomach. Anger stomps it out and dances on its dying ember.

"You had no right to speak for me this morning."

His eyes grow wide. "I'm sorry, Julie. I was just trying to look out for you."

"I don't need you to look out for me."

He drops his head. "I heard you crying last night. I guess I just thought sleeping in and getting more rest would help you feel better."

I take a deep breath to temper the words that want to spill over. "Look, I appreciate your concern. But it is not okay to speak for me. We barely know each other."

His response is long in coming. The air stops moving as he lifts his gaze to meet mine. "I thought we had a connection."

Oh no, he felt the electricity too. It wasn't just my overactive imagination and my dormant-but-waking lust. "I'm married."

His voice drops to a conspiratorial whisper, lined with a crooked grin. "You didn't say happily, Julie."

Maybe not. Heat rushes my cheeks, thoughts swirling around like boiling water. I'm tempted, yes. But I love my husband, and I love my God. *Lord, help me know what to say.* "I don't know about you, Brant, but I am here for one reason and one reason only. To serve God, in a Godly way." I spring to my feet and turn my back to him, lowering my voice to the octave my kids call Mommy's serious tone. "Do not speak for me again."

My legs are shaky as I resist running from him around the corner. I need seclusion, a chance to catch my breath and stem the flow of tears threatening. *I'm so sorry, Adam. For my lustful thoughts and longings that are sinful.*

You need to tell him, Julie. Confession is good for the soul.

I can't, Lord. He will hate me.

He loves you. More than you think.

I press my back to the cool cinderblock wall behind the school house. What have I done to my marriage? Just because Adam cheated on me years ago does not make my thoughts now okay. I thought I forgave him, but maybe that's the root of all my issues. Am I harboring bitterness? Resentment? Unforgiveness, the ultimate of sins?

My tears have left me drained. I snort. Drained. Literally. In this relentlessly hot country, I've never sweated so much. I don't think I've cried this much since I found out about Adam's affair, either. Maybe my body is purging the toxins. But I can't slake my thirst no matter how much water I drink, and crying sure didn't help things. I swipe my cheeks on my already moist shirtsleeve and take a deep breath. I've shared the wall with one of the brown lizards that have become a commonplace sight over the last couple days. He cocks his head to the side, flicks his tongue, and snags a fly from the bumpy concrete blocks. His little throat puffs as he swallows. And a glaze of contentment steals over his glossy eyes. Can lizards look content? I chuckle.

The call for dinner from the sweet kitchen ladies rings into my hiding place. If I don't make a presence, people will believe I really am sick like Brant said this morning. I just hope my face isn't as red and my eyes aren't as puffy as they feel. Brant will think all I do is cry. Who am I kidding? This really is the most frequently I have cried in a long time.

"Bye, little guy." My voice startles the lizard, and he skitters for the nearest bush.

Everyone else is already in the kitchen as I try to slip in unnoticed.

Mam Blessica takes my elbow. "Are you okay?"

I nod and force myself to not focus on the issues simmering under the surface. "I just miss my family." Not a lie.

"I understand. God will bless you for your sacrifice, Julie. I'm happy to have a new friend from America too." She squeezes my waist and wanders toward the rest of the group, now lounging in chairs and on the pavilion.

Anna offers me a coconut drink, today's special treat, and a smile as I fill my plate. Outside, I find a seat as far away from Brant as I can without making a spectacle of the fact that I'm trying to avoid him.

"This food is delicious," Liza mumbles with a mouthful of *pancet*, a scrumptious Filipino noodle dish we are discovering.

"Mm-hmm," I reply. It's true. With pork medallions, onions, and cabbage, this is one of the best things I've ever put in my mouth.

We are all seated around the gazebo with our overflowing plates on our knees. Anna is apparently an amazing cook as well.

"I didn't expect this at all," Lewis says.

"Me either," Brant responds.

Me neither. I stuff another fantastic bite into my mouth and raise my glance to the courtyard where the children are eating. What are they being served? I wrinkle my brow and squint. Rice and beans. And each one has a smile on his or her face.

My appetite vanishes.

We are being treated like kings and queens. Another testimony of our being spoiled. Yes, our mission trip money bought the food, but why should we be eating so well when the children we are here to help are eating like paupers. My stomach turns and threatens nausea.

No one else seems to notice the disparity. Should I feel guilty? Is it an honor to cook so well for us and serve us such bounty?

I sip my coconut smoothie, made from fresh milk, fresh coconut, and some sort of brown sugar harvested locally, plus ice, which is a luxury here, Anna has informed us. It is heavenly too. But I don't deserve this kind of treatment. I came here to be humble. To be a servant. Not to be served.

"Anyone else feel a little badly?" I say with a shaky voice.

All five sets of our team's eyes raise and look at me. Their chewing stops.

"About what?" Dot says.

I nod toward my plate and then toward the children. It seems like they move in slow motion, turning their heads and widening their eyes as realization dawns. I watch as their reactions mirror my own. Chewing stops. Forks go down. Heads bow.

"What do you think they do with our leftovers?" Liza asks.

An idea takes shape. Maybe if we ate less, they would offer the leftovers to the kids. But there are so many of them, surely even with the surplus we leave it wouldn't be enough to feed all of them.

One by one, the gang resumes eating, more subdued than before. I don't know what to do either. I don't want to hurt any feelings, but the next meal I will definitely be serving myself a smaller portion.

My phone ringing makes me jump. I pull it from my backpack. A Facetime call from Adam! I excitedly press the green circle. Eleanor's face appears, grinning ear to ear.

"Hi, Mommy!"

Spontaneous tears spring to my eyes. Oh, great. More crying. I try to swallow the lump in my throat before I speak. "Hi, baby. How are you?"

"Great! Nana took us to McDonald's, and I got a milkshake and an apple pie. And then we played on the playground. And she bought us extra Happy Meal toys."

I chuckle. "Of course she did. That's fantastic. How are your brother and sister?"

"They're good. We miss you, Mommy." Eleanor's smile fades. "When will you be home?"

"Seven more days, I'm afraid." The tears I was barely managing to keep in escape and pour down my cheeks. It's different seeing her sad little face than just hearing her voice.

"Oh."

"I love you, Eleanor."

"I love you too."

I sniffle. "Where's Daddy?"

"Giving Porter a bath. Want to talk to him?"

Yes. No. It's too hard. I want to see all of their faces, but I am not sure I can handle it. I'm barely holding in sobs as it is. I look around the gazebo. It's obvious everyone is trying to mind their own business, but I'm hard to ignore, I imagine.

Liza looks up and smiles sheepishly. An understanding passes between us. She knows how my mommy heart feels, and she doesn't fault me for it.

"No, it's okay, baby. Give them all kisses for me."

"Okay, Grace stayed with Nana for a sleepover anyway. I didn't want to stay. I'm keeping your spot warm, like you said."

I hiccup back another onslaught of tears. "Thank you. That means a lot to me." It feels like too long before I will be able to snuggle her. Too long until I will be able to hold them all.

Liza squeezes my hand as I say goodbye and disconnect the call.

"She was in tears because she misses me. This is so hard."

"I can imagine, Julie. It's okay to be sad and miss them. But remember why you're here. God called you to something special."

I smile. I know. This moment will pass. We will all survive. But the ache in my chest is almost debilitating.

I love siesta time. I never quite understood it back home. But here it is a necessity. I lean against the headboard and open my laptop. The cool air blowing on me dries the remnant drops from my cold shower. I've never been one to shower twice a day. But here this, too, seems to be a necessity.

My eyelids are heavy. Still battling jet lag and heat and mild dehydration, no doubt. It's only 1:00 PM here, so that means Adam and the kids are snug and warm in their beds. I long to call them, but maybe some all-alone, no-temptation-to-call meditation time is good for me.

How long has it been since I had a moment when my loved ones weren't aware of exactly where I am? While it's comforting to have someone who cares about my whereabouts, the freedom—imagined or not—feels pretty good. I am not going to be interrupted. Needed for diapers or meals. Bothered by laundry. Barked at by hungry dogs.

I sink a little deeper into the layer of pillows at my back. Now is the perfect time to compose my thoughts and send my parents, siblings, and Maggie an email. Adam has been updating them, but I've yet to have two seconds to do it myself.

The hotel's Wi-Fi is surprisingly strong, considering I'm sitting in the middle of a third-world jungle. Even my Facebook notifications pop up on the corner of my screen. What could a little social media time hurt?

I click on the notice and am redirected to Facebook, where a picture my mom posted with the kids at McDonald's greets me. She tagged it #missingMomma, but #stillsmiling. I have the best mom in the world. The kids look perfectly placated with ice cream mustaches and French fry grease on their cheeks. Good.

The bell icon says I have fifteen updates. The third one on the list is something from a fellow church member's page. Maybe pictures of the kids from Sunday school will be there somewhere.

My heart drops as the photo opens. It's not the kids. It's Adam. Smiling in the background like he's won the lottery with his arm looped over another woman's shoulders. Obviously caught unawares. And just who is that? I lean closer to the screen and tilt my head. Kristin Lockhart?

Ugh. Her long, blonde hair and trim waist look wonderful in a summery, too-short dress. I've never even seen Adam talk to her, let alone know her well enough to touch her. What is he thinking?

I'm overreacting. I have to be.

My heart begins to pound. Images I've long tried to forget flash before my mind's eyes. Adam with another woman. A blonde from his work. All the pain he inflicted five years ago. Haven't we moved past that? Haven't I healed and forgiven?

He's cheating on me again.

The thought sneaks in the cracks around the edges of my faith in my husband. He promised never to threaten our marriage again. Surely he wouldn't. Would he?

Am I a fool? I let my guard down. Trusted him when I shouldn't have. And I left and opened the door for them to spend as much time together as they like while I'm on the other side of the world.

I feel like that ugly fly the lizard ingested earlier. Stuck. Suffocating.

Tossing the laptop onto the bed next to me, I curl my head in between my knees and squeeze my arms around my shins. My breaths hurt, they are coming so fast and hard.

Just when I started to feel like the walls would tumble, I'm adding another layer. This time reinforced steel. Black. Impenetrable.

Chapter Ten

"He's so good with the kids," Liza leans over and says in a low voice.

I have been staring. My cheeks flush as I turn my gaze away from Brant. "He is." You would think someone so muscly couldn't be so gentle. Yet the children are gathered around him with smiles and giggles, and there's a toddler in his arms.

"I wish James were like that."

I jerk my gaze her direction.

A lovely shade of pink tinges her face, making her all the more beautiful. "I shouldn't have said that. He was great with our children, and that's what matters most. Right?"

James is in deep conversation with Pastor Joel under the canopy of the mango tree. I came to minister to the children, and I hadn't considered that the others in the group might have different purposes here. "That's right." My voice drops. "Adam is very short-tempered with our kids. In fact, it was one of my main arguments with God about asking me to come here." Did I really just confess that out loud?

"Men are very different from us momma bears, aren't they?"

He's cheating on me again, so yeah, you could say that. "Yes." I bite my tongue. The Bible says thoughts of other people outside a marriage are considered adultery. So, technically, with the thoughts I've been having, I am cheating too. But it's not the same as following through with physical actions. Though I long to have someone to vent to, I can't bring myself to say it out loud.

"I have to go to the bathroom." She sighs. "And I don't want to have to go to the bathroom."

I giggle, thankful for the topic change. "I know. It's rather . . . challenging, isn't it?"

"Challenging is not the word for that monstrosity." She rises. "Wish me luck."

"Good luck." I can't say I blame her. As much as my body needs hydration, I am having a hard time drinking because I know it will mean trips to the seatless, flushless, paperless, incredibly short toilet. The one that is even more astounding—not in a flattering way—than the airport's lavatory. *Lord, I will never, ever again take American bathrooms for granted.*

Without my directing it to, my gaze travels back to Brant, who is cooing to the dark-eyed boy in his arms. How sweet.

How sexy.

Oh brother. Here we go again.

But, if Adam is cheating with that blonde-haired beauty, couldn't I—

No. Absolutely not. I refuse to stoop to Adam's level.

Brant glances up and smiles at me. My heart does its annoying flutter thing. Why *does* it have to do that? It apparently doesn't remember that we are mad at Brant. My own organs are betraying me. Great.

As I settle into the same plastic chair I occupied for morning worship, I grab the reins of my flying-into-a-deadly-canyon imagination and desperately try to pull them to a stop. I have to quit obsessing over what I don't know. I glance at my cell phone. Adam should be waking up right about now. He used all of his vacation time in order for me to come.

He sacrificed family time or a vacation this summer for me. I have to find a way to rope my thoughts into submission.

Does he work with Kristin, and I just never realized it? Surely she would have said hi to us at church if she did. Unless she's trying to avoid him because . . .

Ugh. I groan and shift onto the other cheek, both of which are sore from the planes and bus rides. Focus on the plastic flowers shifting in the slight breeze.

Liza slides into the seat next to me, with James on her heels and holding her hand. "You okay?" she whispers.

No. I'm a raving madwoman on the inside who is half a world away and can't figure out if I'm crazy to think Adam's having another affair. I sigh. "Yeah. Just tired."

The audience grows quiet as Pastor Joel takes the stage. "I want to welcome, from our farthest mission church, Brother Samuel, with tonight's message. He is one of our newer churches yet already making a difference for his congregants."

Samuel takes the microphone and smiles with a tinge of a blush on his cheeks. "God is good."

"All the time!" the church responds.

I jump. Yet, their enthusiasm is intoxicating.

"All the time."

"God is good," they chorus even louder.

With these simple words, I can feel the weight of the stress over Adam melting away. Like rough bark shagging off an old oak tree. I sit up a little straighter, feeling the spirit begin to move in the place.

"The Bible tells us that God is the one and only best discerner of spirits. Amen?"

"Amen," I answer quietly.

"First Corinthians 2:15 says, 'But he that is spiritual judgeth all things.' Not he that is carnal. Not he that is intelligent. Or emotional. Or lovely. None of our human qualities can ascertain the way the spirit of God inside us can.

"How can we approach situations with the peace and calm that God provides?" Samuel pauses for several dramatic seconds.

I know the answer already. I've been ignoring this very advice all day.

"We come to it in our spiritual bodies, without bringing our hurt feelings or past experiences into the matter. We come with humbleness, asking God—not man, not myself—to reveal the full truth of the situation. Only He can help you know which friends are genuine, which preaching is real, which man is telling the truth.

"Remember, with God all things are possible. That doesn't mean He wants you to take matters into your own hands because you can't fail. No, you can fail. What He means is that if you cling to His wisdom and power, you will see Him succeed."

Samuel's words are piercing through that outer layer of armor I erected earlier, like a giant's spike peeling a tin can. It aches, and it's slow, but in this moment it is unavoidable. I bow my head. As the world around me fizzles away, the words of my heart begin to pour forth like silent tears. *Lord, I don't trust Adam, but I trust You. Reveal to me the truth, Your truth. And give me confidence to believe in reality instead of the falsities and fears I want to cave to. Hold me up. Allow me to speak with Adam soon, so we can clear the air. Protect my children while I'm gone. Protect my heart, Lord, please.*

Daet at night is beautiful. Still terribly hot, but at least when the sun goes down it isn't sizzling. A sort of quiet steals over the rice fields as the *carabao*, another Filipino term I learned from George for the water buffalo-like cattle, and their long-legged, white stork friends settle in. I haven't seen any snakes, but I am sure they are somewhere, slithering beneath the wilted tips of the grass to feast on the numerous mice and sparrows I've seen in every setting. Maybe even those little lizards. No wonder they tend to stay at the tops of the walls. Or, I chuckle, maybe that's because the naked bulbs attract their dinners. Duh.

The breeze blowing into the trike smells less like exhaust at this time, too, making my lips and gums thankfully less tingly.

"You okay?" Liza asks, squished against the inner wall next to me.

"Hmm? Oh, yes. Just ready to call and talk to my family."

"I understand. James," she points to his legs dangling near our heads, his body obstructed by the silver metal of the sidecar cage, "asked me earlier if your children were okay without you. He mentioned how you look at the littles here with such longing."

"Do I?"

"Mm-hmm. Only natural, Momma."

"I do miss them terribly." But right now that's not what's consuming my thoughts. I need the sanctuary of my room before I crack open the tender-shelled eggs I fear I might be trampling. Do I even want to know the truth while I'm so far from home? It's not like I can get back and do a thing about it.

"You're a good mom, Julie. Even here. Think of it this way—you are giving your beautiful babies a wonderful example to follow. As much as you miss them, and as hard as it was to leave them, you are following God's plan for you. I think it's just wonderful."

I tilt my head and swipe at the stray hairs tickling my forehead. "I hadn't looked at it that way before."

"It's true." She sighs. "So what did you think of your class today?"

A broad smile stretches my lips. "I want to take every single one of them home."

"Me too. They are so precious. And don't you think there's such an innocence here we don't see at home anymore?"

"Completely agree. I never realized how much of a blessing a lack of electronics would be. No half-naked teenagers on television for the girls to model themselves after.

No cool, backward-hatted, doped up teens for the boys to follow. It's wonderful."

Liza vigorously nods, her humid-frizzy hair bouncing along.

"There's so much I want to change when I get home."

"Me too."

My throat is tired of yelling over the sound of the whooshing air. I'm just tired in general, though. But it's a different tired. A good tired. A clean-out-your-pores, worked-hard-all-day kind of tired. How long has it been since I've had a day where I didn't mediate at least one fight? Clean up at least one mess? Or have to put at least one child in time-out?

As we near the hotel, my heart begins to climb higher into my throat. Almost there. Almost time to call Adam and ask the question I've been dreading but needing the answer to all day.

I'm so consumed in my inner turmoil, I don't even notice Brant on my heels until I reach to open the lock and hear him shuffling right behind me. I spin and clasp my hand to my chest. "You almost gave me a heart attack, Brant. What are you doing?"

He looks at his shoes. "I wanted to apologize. Again. For earlier."

It takes a minute to register. This morning seems a lightyear away already. And I've had bigger worries crash into my orbit since then. I take a deep breath before I answer. "You know what? It's okay. I know you didn't mean to hurt me."

He sighs. "I really didn't. You were absolutely right that I overstepped my bounds. I mean, we barely know each other. I had no right to speak for you. I promise it will never happen again." He wiggles his eyebrows. "Unless you want it to, that is."

I scowl and open my mouth to berate him.

"I'm just kidding, Julie." He touches my elbow. "I've been lonely a long time and clearly I misread the situation. Forgive me?"

Boy, I'd sure like to. If only he would remove the electrifying excitement his fingertips are shooting into my body. I take a step back, but I have nowhere to go. For an instant, my gaze drops to his lips.

No.

I force my eyes to focus on his. "Right, well I'd better turn in. I need to call my husband." I take care to enunciate the last two words, making sure he understands the boundaries. Making sure I do.

"Good night, Julie."

The huskiness in his voice is doing strange things to my kneecaps. "Night." I fumble with the key in the lock and hurry into my room in reverse. Why does he have to be so blame handsome? And right next door.

I slide the thin glass door open to my incredibly narrow balcony. There's barely enough room for me to step onto it. I peek over the rail below before I squeeze the excess water from the clothes I just washed in the sink. Also tiny. Hard to do with shampoo too. I'm going to have to remember to ask Blessica tomorrow about a laundry service.

Surely I packed enough, I remember thinking as I stared at the two massive suitcases on my bedroom floor before I left. I hadn't planned on two outfits a day because of the sweaty nature of my used-to-air-conditioning pores.

A frog of some sort makes a birdlike call from a nearby tree. Well, I think it's a frog since I can't see a bird. But what do I know about the wildlife here? The tops of the coconut trees stand perfectly still under the pall of the humid blanket that is the normal air in the Philippines, apparently.

Yet, there is still such beauty. Am I really here? In the tropic Southeast Asian country whose people are friendly and kind and the countryside is filled with lovely hues of green. A million worlds away from my family and whatever it is Adam is doing with his arm around Blondie's shoulder.

I yank out my phone and dial home. No more agonizing over this issue. The phone rings and rings. And rings. Voicemail. The bland, deeper-than-normal message telling me to leave a message.

This isn't something that can be left on voicemail.

Where in the world are they this morning? I don't remember them having plans. None that I laid out, anyway. Maybe Mom came by and took them somewhere.

I fall onto the bed with a humph. Great. Now I have to sleep with this worry gnawing a hole in me like an ulcer in my mind. I pull up the photo a second time. And immediately wish I hadn't. How exactly had I thought that would help anything? The ten intent seconds I inspect it tell me nothing additional and only add to the boiling-blood feeling in my veins.

Slamming my phone on the nightstand, I flip off the bedside lamp. Tomorrow is coming. And I don't want to spend it lost in the sin of my worrying. A tear trickles down my cheek, pooling in my ear. *Lord, please help me! I hate these walls around my heart. I hate the suspicion and the memories. The padlocks on all the doors that might be able to breach the insurmountable bricks protecting me. Isolating me.*

The thought of strong, willing arms literally a foot from my head pulls my mind toward him. The emptiness inside longs to be comforted. I want to be held. I want someone to talk to, to chase away the intense loneliness aching in my breast. *I wish he would come to my door again.* My ears strain for the sound of any faint knock. Any faint hope that someone can feel my pain and would want to stem the flow.

Nothing.

I swing my feet over the bed and silently plant them on the cool tile. With a deep breath and a few stealthy steps, I find my hand on the door knob and my heart pounding in my throat. Something inside me is screaming, "Get back in bed! This will pass!" But without even pausing, I turn the handle and glide the few feet to Brant's door.

Now what?

Do I really want to do this? Yes.

No.

Ugh. I lean my forehead on the wall and drop the hand I don't remember raising to knock. A jiggle of his door echoes into the hallway. My heart leaps into my mouth.

I turn to flee, slipping into the safety of my room and gently closing the door just as I hear his swing open. That was close.

Leaping onto the mattress, I throw the covers over my head like a kid caught out of bed on Christmas Eve. A nervous chuckle escapes my lips. Who exactly is going to see me pretending to be asleep?

A dark tide sweeps through my conscience. What a hypocrite I am! Hard, hot, angry tears fly from my eyes, each one reminding me that I'm a fool. A selfish, weak fool.

Chapter Eleven

I startle and wake from a nightmare about me and Brant in a lover's embrace. Adam walked in with all three children and caught us. All four of them began to wail, red tears streaming down their faces.

The piece of charcoal sky I can see through the narrowly opened curtain is filled with heavy clouds. Isn't it supposed to be the dry season right now?

The heavy, syrupy glue of guilt still clings to my mind. Did I actually almost knock on Brant's door in the middle of the night? I roll my eyes. I'm such an idiot. I move over and grab my phone from the nightstand. 4:33. No sense in going back to sleep.

No missed calls or messages from Adam either. Didn't he see where he missed my call? Maybe he doesn't care. Maybe he's with *her.*

I throw the now-heavy covers off and stamp my feet to the floor. This is getting me nowhere. My imagination is running away on its own. Grabbing my Bible and plopping it in my lap, it falls open to Psalm 147, one of my favorites.

"He telleth the number of the stars; he calleth them all by their names."

That's right. God knows every detail. He can see the whole world right now. Wherever Adam is, wherever my children are, He can see. He is watching over them. Keeping them safe. Hopefully keeping Adam from doing anything stupid.

And He can see me too. And knows my thoughts. Oh how I wish I could shield them from His piercing eyes. I drop my chin to my chest.

Lord, help me focus on Your will in my life today. Keep me from worry. Help me help someone else. And keep my mind from places it shouldn't go.

After several deep breaths with slow exhales, I can feel the tension from the nightmare ebbing away.

"We started the feeding program in Mercedes about six months ago," Blessica informs us as we bounce along a rutted dirt road.

The Jeepney groans into a lower gear to climb a steep hill, and my bottom slides several inches farther rearward on the silver bench seat. I grab the windowsill and right myself, glancing at the others. Everyone but Blessica is struggling not to slide out the open back door. Brant catches my gaze and flashes a shy smile.

What is he thinking? Heat flares in my chest. Does he know it was me outside his room last night? That I almost ruined my marriage and crossed a line I swore I'd never even approach? Loneliness is serious business, isn't it? I don't think I've ever experienced it before, not really. I've never lived on my own. Never been abandoned by a loved one or left for more than a few hours alone. These empty-room nights are good for me. I'm learning a new aspect of life, learning how to empathize with others. And learning how blessed I am to be surrounded by family back home. But what if I am not strong enough to resists its ugly pull? What if I do something enormously stupid?

I moan as we bounce over another bump and turn my attention to the fields and forests zipping by the window.

I wonder once more, why did I think the devil would stop fighting me about this trip once I boarded the plane? Of course he is still waging war. We are working for Him, and Satan hates it.

Well, I straighten my shoulders and thrust my chin a few inches higher, I won't let him win. Not when I was struggling with the idea of leaving my family. Not now. Not ever.

"Are you tired, dear?" Blessica pats my hand and presses her lips together.

"Oh, please forgive me." I place my hand atop hers. "I was lost in another world. What were you saying about the feeding program?"

"The children here are just precious. We have seen many of them come to Christ. Today will be so special, with their families coming too." The compressed line of her lips grows into a wide smile. "We hope to see thirty souls saved today."

And there it is. The definite difference between her thoughts and mine. Between this blooming birth of new belief in Jesus and the worn-out, petty version of church I've seen back home. Where the people here truly devote their lives wholeheartedly to missions, to soul-winning, every minute of every day, we argue over carpet colors and thermostat settings. And get our feelings hurt when someone sits in our pew. And let our thoughts constantly wander to selfishness. Oh, woe is me! I've been thinking of nothing but myself, it seems, since I got here.

Here I am worrying about my husband and letting that unfounded dread nearly consume me. I almost did something so unforgivable, I'd be ashamed to say it out loud. I should be focused on the Lord with every breath and thought. Not everyone gets to experience something so wonderful. Such an opportunity to travel across the world and teach others about the abundant love of Jesus.

I will focus on Him. From this moment on. No more thoughts of muscly co-missionaries. No more thoughts of trim blondes. God has a plan. It is for my good. And I will stop worrying. I nod, punctuating my internal monologue.

The Jeepney comes to a slow halt in front of a plain white, block church. No glass decorates the windows. No doors hang in the hinges.

"We're here!" Blessica practically leaps from the cab.

A horde of children with smudged faces and bare feet come barreling around the corner and draw up short when they spot the six Americans exiting the tiny Jeepney door. Their eyes grow wide, and their mouths seal up tighter than Ziplocs.

My heart instantly warms. Expectant faces line up outside the church door, at the open windows, vying for a position closest to the "rich" Americans who have come to teach them about Jesus today. And feed them.

My stomach lurches remembering the extravagant breakfast we were served. Meat, eggs, fresh fruit, coffee with sugar and cream. These babies are happy with the pot of vegetable soup and one tiny roll each of them will receive. *Lord, there is so much need here!*

The men carry in the gigantic black kettle of soup prepared by the women of the home church this morning. The one they made while they simultaneously spoiled us spoiled missionaries. I settle into a rickety plastic chair at the front of the one-room church and take in the scene. The ladies involved in the feeding program have been here often—they don't need our help whatsoever. But it is a blessing to be witness to this humbling moment. My children have never gone hungry. Not a day in their life. Never gone without access to Pop-Tarts and chocolate milk.

When I return home, I will find room in our budget to support this ministry. *I promise, Lord.*

Our budget. Will there be an "our" when I return? Humph. Will there be an "our" after I finally manage to have a phone conversation with Adam?

A dark-haired girl of about three plops into my lap, dribbling soup onto my skirt. "*Salamat, po,*" she manages between bites.

I shake my head. No thoughts of marriage troubles today. None. "You're welcome, sweetie." Wrapping my arms around her, I let my eyes slide closed. God has a plan for me. There's a reason I'm here, and I don't want to miss it with morbid, self-centered thoughts. "Is your soup good?"

"Mm-hmm." More reddish juice splashes onto my skirt as she spins to wrap me in a sweaty hug.

I am so blessed to be here. In this moment. For this purpose.

"Are you ready to begin the lesson, *Mam* Julie?" Dot asks.

Wait. What? I've heard the men joking about "throwing each other under the bus" while they've been here. Calling on each other to unplanned tasks. For a single heartbeat, I consider feigning an illness or something to avoid another public speaking engagement. But my usual guttural response isn't manifesting. No twinges of sharp pain in my abdomen. No profuse—well, not spontaneous, uncalled-for, anyway—sweating. No shaking cells that quiver until my entire body has trouble being still. *Instant in* season. I take a deep breath and nod. "Sure. Do you have anything in particular in mind?"

"Tell them about Jesus."

"My pleasure."

"Okay, children, gather round! *Mam* Julie has a story to share with you."

Children of all ages, their dark eyes wide with anticipation, gather at my skirt hem. Even the teenagers seem excited to hear the words I will speak. *Lord, I'm ready. Show me what to teach.* An idea ignites, and a smile spreads over my face. "Do you know what it means to be 'instant in season'?"

"Hi, Mommy." Porter's voice is slurred like his mouth is full of peanut butter.

A heavy sigh escapes me. Thank goodness they finally answered. I was getting ready to call in the Nana Calvary. "Hey, buddy. What are you doing up so early?"

"We slept with Daddy so we wouldn't miss it if you called."

I giggle. "Oh, that's good. I miss all of you so much." I feel the tears filling my eyes, emotion constricting my throat. I should be in that overcrowded bed with our morning breath and stretches. "I wish I could give you each a big ole hug."

"Me too. Ms. Susan came by yesterday morning. She brought us cookies and movie tickets! Daddy said we can go this weekend and see something."

"That was so nice of her." *Thank you, Lord, for a wonderful church family and for Susan's kindness.*

"She told me to tell you . . . umm . . . oh, yeah! That the women's class is praying for you every Sunday."

So, everyone hasn't forgotten me. "Thank you, Porter. That means a lot to me. I love you. Can I talk to your sisters? I don't have very many international minutes left."

"Love you too."

Eleanor and Grace chat for a moment between giant yawns, equally as excited as Porter about their new upcoming trip to the movies. "Here's Daddy," they both chant at the same time.

My heart skips. Do I ease into the third degree or just dive right in?

"Hey, hon. How was your day?"

"Hot but wonderful. These people are truly amazing. And the preaching! I feel like I'm in revival." If only I hadn't worried so much. My most frequent sin.

"That's good."

"How was group study Wednesday night?"

"Good. It grows every Wednesday."

Good, huh? Just good? "Did the kids go to class okay without me?"

"Yeah. Ms. Lorna bribed them with suckers."

I chuckle. "Of course she did."

He yawns.

As carefree as any man can be. Surely that's not the manner of a guilty conscience. "Anything new going on?"

"Your mom took us to the zoo yesterday."

That's why I couldn't get ahold of him. At least he wasn't doing anything with Kristin. But I worried all day for nothing. Couldn't he have mentioned it or at least shot me a text? "That was nice of her."

"Yeah, we had a good time."

I take a deep breath and choose my words carefully. "I gotta admit, I was getting pretty worried when I couldn't get you on the phone. I really miss home." Tears choke the word home.

"I'm sorry. Home misses you too."

I swallow and try to smile. I need relief from this incessant niggling in the back of my mind. But if I ask these burning questions and begin an argument, all he has to do is hang up and I'll spend another day agonizing. *Lord, what should I do?*

Trust me, Julie. Wait.

Does Adam feel the awkwardness that has crept into our silence? That never used to happen. Not before the affair. We could be silent in the car together for hours, letting our hands clasped together over the console share unspoken energy.

Adam was a man I never would've envisioned being capable of cheating. I trusted him so completely. Felt so safe in his arms. All it took was one moment of his weakness to shatter that trust, and I've spent five years trying to find it again. I can sense the jabs of anger and resentment creeping up again. Surely this isn't God's plan for this trip, I think for the millionth time. My interrogation can wait for a better time. "Listen, hon, I'd better get some sleep. I have no idea what our Filipino friends have in store for us tomorrow, but I know it will be wonderfully exhausting."

He chuckles. "Okay, get some rest. Love you."

I close my eyes, savoring each word, making sure they hold the power of truth in them. "I love you too."

Chapter Twelve

The lobby is empty. I glance at my watch for the tenth time. I'm early. Still early. My pulse is increasing each time I look at the time. Where is everyone? Surely they didn't leave me again. George is not in his customary stool behind the counter. I take a deep breath, let it out slowly, trying to envision my heart rate slowing. I made it to the school by myself the other day. I can do it again, if need be.

A tap on my shoulder makes me jump. I spin and practically nosedive into Brant's solid chest.

"Mornin'." He smiles.

I take four steps back. "Hi." Tighten my ponytail. "Where is everyone?"

"Didn't you get the text?"

I shake my head and yank out my phone. It's been on silent. Of course. "What's going on?"

"*Mam* Blessica split us into groups for the day. The others left for their day trips earlier." He shrugs. "You and I are going to visit Pastor Antony's church this morning."

My stomach sinks. Seriously, Dot? How can she not sense the tension between me and Brant? "Is he picking us up soon?"

"Should be here any minute."

I fiddle with my phone for a moment. I can't breathe the stuffy lobby air any longer. Outside, I pull up the group texts. At least they did try to inform me of their plans this time.

Okay, Lord, how exactly am I supposed to get through the day practically alone with Brant? Help me out here!

"Did you sleep well?"

His deep voice directly behind me, with the morning sun casting piercing rays through the gray, stirs to life the swirling emotions I've been trying so hard to quench. It is just the two of us in the whole world. In this beautiful side garden filled with exotic pink flowers and tiny birds flitting about. I slowly turn to face him, my neck craning to peer into his face so much taller than mine. "Are you teasing me, Brant?"

"Wouldn't dream of it." His mouth quirks into a half-grin.

He knows. I can see it in his eyes. He knows that I was outside his door. "I slept fine. Thank you."

"Good. Glad to hear it." He takes a sidestep and strolls to the sidewalk, glancing left and right. Casual. Confident.

What have I done? I'm telling him one thing, but my actions are betraying me. I cannot let myself be weak again. Adam is at home with our babies, being a good dad. And I'm not here for an illicit fling. I'm here to serve God.

How many times have I reminded myself of that very thing? There is seriously something wrong with me.

I grab the picture of my family tucked inside my wallet and stare at it. Adam hurt me, yes, but he's apologized. I could never betray my marriage vows. Never. There. That's that.

"Ready, Julie?" Brant shouts.

Pastor Antony has arrived on a trike and is waiting with a broad smile. He waves at me.

I return the wave. Please let Brant ride on the bike. Not the sidecar. Not the sidecar. The men exchange a few words, and Brant hops onto the rack behind the motorcycle, next to the sidecar. Whew. Okay, I can do this.

Gathering my skirt, I jog to them and slip inside the sidecar. It's not too bad to ride in one when it's just one person occupying it. I stretch my legs and arrange my bags. I know Brant is somewhere to my left, but I can't see him. Thankfully.

I can spend the entire drive praying and centering my thoughts on God's will for today.

"This your husband?" a smiling teenage girl approaches and asks me, blushing as she glances toward Brant.

My eyes grow wide. "No," I snap a bit too quickly.

Her smile instantly falls.

"I'm sorry. My husband is back home. Brant is just a friend." I'm not even sure I can call him that with as little as I know about him. But that's easier to explain than "the stranger I'm on a mission trip with."

Her smile returns as she nods vigorously. "Oh. You have children?"

I sigh. An easier topic, for sure. "I do. Three."

"You have a son?"

I chuckle. I've learned from our short time here the teen girls have an exit strategy. A way to escape poverty and a life of hardship. Marry an American. "I do."

She takes a step closer, into my already tight personal bubble. But I've learned that culturally the Filipinos have no bubbles.

"Want to see a picture of him?"

"Yes! He come here too?"

"Maybe someday. He's only two."

"Oh! You were joking with me." Her laughter is sweet, without a thought of self-consciousness.

"Yes, I'm sorry. Still, he is a handsome little guy, don't you think?" I hand the laminated photo to her.

"*Mam* Julie, they are beautiful. You are very blessed."

"I am. This is my husband, Adam." I point to his smiling face.

"He is very handsome too."

I've studied the children's precious faces a hundred times over the past four days, but for the first time I truly take in Adam's. When was the last time I noticed his long lashes and shining eyes? The dimpled chin with a touch of graying stubble. I married a very handsome man, indeed. "Thank you."

She wanders away to visit with her friends, and I am alone again in the corner of Pastor Antony's church. We're waiting for the special service to begin, and I've found the one place that seems to catch a bit of a breeze through the square window to my left.

I have noticed other women noticing Adam, and it used to make me hold my head a bit higher. Somewhere along the line, though, I've forgotten to pay attention. What if Kristin has been doing a better job of that than I have? Making him feel more physically appreciated than I do? I force the thought into a file folder in my mind marked, "Thoughts for Later," and return my attention to the room.

The young woman I was chatting with approaches Brant and giggles as he turns his attention toward her. His deep voice is easy to hear over the crowd. "Hello. How are you today?"

I can't catch her reply, other than the giggling.

"How old are you, Ella?"

Again, her reply is lost in the noise.

"I have a daughter about your age. Would you like to see a photo?"

No matter the personality, parents are all the same, aren't we? I may not know much about Brant, but I do know he is proud of his child. And he's good with the kids here. He is tender hearted, gentle. On a mission trip, so he must be humble too. And obedient to God.

And handsome. Strong.

I bet he never kicked his daughter's toys into the wall or complained when his wife didn't have time to restock the fridge. He probably never made her feel self-conscious about the weight she'd gained by making subtle remarks concerning the calories in snack foods. Or fell asleep when she was telling him about her day. And he most certainly didn't have an affair.

Heat flares in my chest. *Adam can be such a jerk, Lord. Why do I have to put up with that?*

The saying "Tigers can't change their stripes" rears its ugly head. I've always believed anyone is capable of change. But what if it's just another of my naïve wishes? I do tend to find the good in everyone. Even when it isn't there.

Adam may never change. A wave of heavy warmth washes over me. I may have to be miserable in my marriage for the rest of my life. If I were drunk, that thought would sober me right up.

This may be my lot in life. To suffer through feeling lonely, underappreciated, and worthless at the hands of a selfish, uncaring husband. Who is home right now with a gorgeous blonde. And no wife anywhere in sight.

Suddenly, I'm finding it hard to breathe. My heart pounds an irregular beat against my ribs. Leaning over, I bury my head in my hands. And focus on the next breath. And the next. Calm down, Julie, before you make a spectacle of yourself. These people will laugh at your fat, red cheeks if you don't get yourself under control.

A hot hand touches my back. "Julie? Are you okay?"

Brant. Of course. Kind, compassionate Brant. I shake my head without lifting it.

"Come on. Let's get some fresh air." His large palm slides under my elbow, urges me to stand.

He leads me out the side door, pulling me to the welcoming shade beneath a grove of coconut trees. I lean into a trunk and press my eyes closed. Though the breeze feels wonderful, my breaths refuse to deepen.

"I'll get some water," he says.

I peel my eyelids open and watch him jog back to the church. He reappears moments later with two bottles, a frown stretched on his mouth, and hurries back to me. "Here, drink this."

I don't bother to argue. The ice-cold water rinses the sour taste from my mouth. "Thanks."

"What's going on?"

His gaze is so intense, I can hardly meet it. "It's nothing. I'm just overheated."

"I don't buy that, Julie."

I shake my head, but unwanted tears spring to my eyes.

"Is everything okay at home? Your kids?"

No, nothing is okay. I open my mouth, but words don't come out.

"Is it your husband? Is he hurt?"

"Yes," I whisper. "No. He's not hurt. He . . . he . . ." I can't bring myself to voice my fears. A sob rises into my throat, choking me.

"Come here."

I let Brant pull me into his arms. The ones I've thought about incessantly. He wraps me into them, like a warm blanket keeping me from the winter's chill. It feels so good to be protected. To be sheltered. Tension flows out of my shoulders with my tears. I grip his t-shirt with both hands and let them come.

He doesn't speak. Doesn't ask more questions. Doesn't even move. But I can hear his pounding heart and feel the rapid rise and fall of his chest. What am I doing? It should be Adam holding me. This is not my husband. This is not an embrace a married woman should be having.

I pull away and swipe at my tears.

Brant's arms drop to his sides. He swallows hard. "Has he hurt you?"

Yes. I am an emotionally wrecked woman. But I can't have this conversation with Brant. It's too intimate. "No," I say without looking him in the eye. I have to escape his magnetic pull. "Thank you for worrying about me. I'm fine."

He raises an eyebrow.

"Really. I just need a minute. Alone."

"You sure?"

I force myself to smile. "I'm sure. I'll be there in a minute."

When he turns his back, I melt into the tree behind me and sigh. My legs and arms are quivering like the leaves above me under the strong breeze that's kicked up. That was not good. I'm such a weakling! Allowing him to hold me that way . . . and to enjoy it. It's been so long since Adam did that. I cry alone. Locked in the bathroom so the kids don't see. So Adam doesn't worry or feel bad.

The sounds of the congregation singing the opening hymn float through the air. I need to compose myself and rejoin them. *This* is why I'm here. Church. Worship. Praise. Helping others. With my mind re-centered, I swipe one last time at my cheeks, square my shoulders, and return to the humble building.

They've saved me a seat on the front row. Next to Brant.

Figures.

Pastor Antony takes the mic and begins, "Jesus was tempted in the wilderness."

Seriously, Lord? Are you preaching to anyone *besides me on this trip?*

I can't help but think God has a mighty big sense of humor. And irony. I scooch a few more centimeters away from the heat radiating from Brant's side.

Antony reads Matthew chapter four and launches into his message. "We are all tempted to sin from time to time. Alcohol, lust, drugs, slothfulness. All of them are part of this world, but we must refrain. We are to set ourselves aside as special. Different. Because someone is always watching us, and the way we live our lives either shines a light for God or adds more darkness to this world."

Oh boy. Drive a stake right on into my fragile fortress. I am fidgeting. I know it. I can't seem to make my mind or body still.

Brant smiles at me.

Innocent enough. But there's something in his eyes. More than simple concern. More than simple friendship.

I must be imagining things. I shut down those improper thoughts when we talked. Right?

I roll my eyes. Like I'm doing such a wonderful job of shutting them down in my own mind. We do have a connection. I can't deny it. It isn't based on knowing everything about each other, long conversations into the middle of the night, or common interests. It's an undeniable electrical spark. Scratch that. More like an arc. A burning, dazzling, distracting arc of energy bolting from something inside him to meet something inside me.

I must turn it off.

I must find a way to rise above temptation. Jesus was perfect, so of course he could ignore the devil in the wilderness. *Lord, what do You want me to do? How do I kill this reaction to a man I barely know?*

Get to know him.

I almost laugh out loud. *That's a great plan, Lord.* Was I just sarcastic with the God of the universe? Is actual lightning going to strike me? I squirm to the far edge of my seat. Any farther and I will be in the floor. *I'm sorry, but You can't be serious. I need distance. Not more to like him for.*

No response. But Antony is hopping up and down on stage. Punctuating his words on the down steps. "The only way to overcome temptation is to face it head on, meet it with resolve, and knock it into next week."

Okay, I get it. Get to know Brant. Make the "friends" statement truth. Easy enough.

Not.

Chapter Thirteen

Ella slips into the furnace of a trike car beside me.

She takes up so much less room than I do. "Are you excited about the baptism?"

She nods.

"Nervous?"

"A little. I'm afraid of the ocean."

"I've never been to a saltwater baptism before, but I have been swimming. You will be okay."

"*Salamat, po.*"

Brant hops onto the rack, Pastor Antony drives, and soon we are flying along dirt pathways in a general easterly direction. I think. It's hard to tell when I can't see out the windows or am even in the same hemisphere as normal.

As we pull to a stop, Brant offers his hand to Ella and me, helping us both squeeze from the tiny space. I lift my eyes and take in the surroundings, speechless. I saw the ocean from the air, but nothing could compare to the view before me now. Turquoise water laps onto light brown sand. Palm and coconut trees sway in a fresh breeze. Tiny, nearly invisible ghost crabs dart between hiding holes. Volcanoes rise from the blue horizon, watching over the picturesque bay. It looks like a postcard.

I feel suddenly conspicuous, like someone is watching me. Brant is frozen in his tracks, smiling at me with a look I've not seen before. "What?"

"You're beautiful, Julie. Inside and out."

As if he didn't mean to say the words out loud, he swipes a hand over his mouth and trots to catch up with the group making their way down to the beach.

I'm beautiful? His words find a mark I didn't know was being ignored. Adam tells me sometimes, and it's nice to hear, but somehow Brant's compliment means more.

Tempted in the wilderness. I brush aside a tendril of some sort of fern on the trail to the beach. I'm definitely in the wilderness. And I'm definitely tempted. I need to talk to Adam. It's so easy to feel that I'm in a world separate from them and my actions won't have consequences when they are so far away.

But I know better.

The last thing I want to do is hurt Adam the way he hurt me. I'm better than that. And there will never be a chance for us to completely heal if I make this mistake now. Thoughts are one thing. Actions a whole other beast. And as soon as I talk to Adam, I can clear the air. Both of my guilt-ridden conscience and my worry. There. Case closed. Again.

The late-morning sun glints off the waves, sand squishy beneath my sandals. Pastor Antony wades into the water and turns to face us, his huge smile beaming at our small group still on the beach. "This is a blessed day. Sister Ella, brother Amniel, please join me."

I give Ella's hand a squeeze. She and the young man, Amniel, slip into the water and soon the three of them are emerging, soaking wet and grinning broadly. A short, simple ceremony, but it means so much to these people. To me. Will my own babies decide to make this step in their faith someday? I pray so.

There is no room with towels and dry clothes waiting for the newly baptized teens. Yet they seem unperturbed by the idea of riding home drenched.

Riding home drenched . . . Ella rode here with me in the sidecar.

"*Mam* Julie, you can ride with Brother Brant on Amniel's bike. Okay?" Pastor Samuel smiles.

"No, um, it's okay. I don't mind getting wet. I'll ride in the sidecar with Ella. No problem." I'm rambling, but just as my thoughts were headed this direction, he has voiced them, and I cannot be alone with Brant. Not now.

"We insist," he continues. "Brant has his license back home, he told me. So it will be safe. Ella and Amniel can ride with me in the trike. It will be good, no?"

I don't want to disappoint this kind pastor, but there is *no way* I am getting on the back of the motorcycle with my legs flung over the sides, in a skirt, behind Brant. Besides, I don't even like motorcycles, and there are no helmets here. "I'm not dressed properly."

"Like this, *Mam* Julie." Pastor Antony hops on the rear seat sidesaddle and grins.

"I promise to drive safely. Scouts honor." Brant holds up the customary two fingers.

Oh, for Pete's sake. Does no one understand?

Pastor Antony, Ella, and Amniel make their way to the trike, matters settled, apparently.

Brant is staring at me again. "You okay?"

"I just don't like motorcycles very much."

"You've been riding on one all week."

"I have been riding *next* to one all week."

He wrinkles his brow and quirks a crooked smile.

I chuckle. "All right, I get it."

The others are chatting in a bunch a short distance away. "I hope we leave soon, I'm starving."

"Anna's lunch sounds like it would hit the spot right about now."

"Definitely." Food, safe topic. Children, also safe. "So, tell me about your daughter. We've not had much time to talk since we've been here."

A genuine smile spreads his lips. "I think I mentioned that she's thirteen."

I nod.

"But, now don't tell anyone I said this or it might jinx things, she isn't very teenagery."

"That's not a word." I smile.

He laughs. "You know what I mean. Everyone said the teen years would be hard, but I'm very blessed. She is a wonderful, caring, smart young lady."

"Does she stay with you much?"

"Most of the time. She only goes to her mother's every other weekend."

"That's unusual." I clap a hand to my mouth. "Sorry, I didn't mean to say that out loud."

"It's okay. It is unusual. Her mother has some issues. I didn't know about them until after we had Laney." He runs a hand over his jawline.

"It's really none of my business. You don't have to tell me."

"Laney won a speech contest last month."

Good, away from the ex-wife category. "That's amazing. I hate public speaking." I frown. "Well, I did before I came, anyway. Everything's different here."

He pierces me with one of those smoldering, intense stares again. "It is."

My turn to steer things to safer waters. "My little ones have straight A's in Sunday School. Does that count as impressive?"

A deep chuckle erupts from him. "It is remarkable. You should be proud, really."

"I'm their teacher."

His laughter is contagious, and I find myself giggling.

"Time to go!" Pastor Antony shouts.

"Come on." Brant hops on the motorcycle and starts it.

I basically have no other options, other than walking back. And I have no idea where I'm going. I climb onto the back seat, wrap my hand around the bar at the back, and squeeze my eyes shut. *Lord, please don't let me die on this contraption.*

"Ready?"

I nod my head and scoot a little farther from Brant's back. As he begins to move, I lurch backward, but once we are on the road, I can feel my body adjusting to the motion. The breeze is much better outside of the sidecar, and for the first time in my life, I'm enjoying a motorcycle ride. No helmet. Adam wouldn't believe it.

With my skirt whipping around my ankles and my muscles relaxing a bit, I am free to take in the grandeur of the country. I hadn't been able to notice on the drive in how we passed a volcano in the distance, rising sharply at the back of a long field. Or how colorful shirts hung to dry in open windows and smoke curled from piles of burning rice husks. I could stay here forever. Awash in contentment, on this peaceful island, far removed from technology and soccer practice and doctor's appointments. If my family were here, I imagine I could have a sense of serenity I've never before been able to maintain.

What if we did become full-time missionaries here?

The thought makes me sit a little straighter. My arm presses against Brant's sweaty back. I instantly recoil. But no sparks are rocketing from my skin. Good. Maybe this get to know him better thing is working?

What issues does his ex-wife have? Drugs? Alcohol? Surely not. But if it was serious enough for him to have full custody, it must be something intense.

Brant pulls into the home church, and as soon as the bike stops rolling, I hop to my feet. I'm sad the ride is over but thankful to put some distance between us. Dot waves from the kitchen doorway. I need to talk to her. How do I request not to be alone with Brant again, without revealing my attraction for him?

I take a deep breath and draw on my courage. "Can we talk, Dot?"

"Of course. Everything okay?"

I nod and put my empty plate on the bench beside me. The others have meandered toward the pavilion to wait for rides back to the hotel. "I am not sure it is good for me to be alone with Brant."

Her eyebrow arches. "Oh?"

What is my excuse? Oh! "I don't think it looks right. A single man and a married woman. And we are around the same age. I'm afraid people will think he is my husband."

She exhales. "Thank goodness. I was afraid you were going to say something happened." She pats my hand. "I'm sorry I didn't think of that sooner. You are absolutely right."

I let go the breath I've been holding. "Thank you."

Nap time. Lovely, cool, wonderful nap time. I've always loved naps, when I could manage to snag one, but I've never appreciated them as I do now.

It's two in the morning back home. No sense in trying to call home, so I sink into my pillows and let my eyelids fall closed.

The ringing of my phone on the nightstand makes my heart skip. "Who in the world?" I grab it and hit the green button without really looking at the number. "Hello?"

"Julie? It's Maggie."

It feels amazing hearing my best friend's voice. "What are you doing up so late?"

"I wanted to call you."

My insides warm. "I'm so glad you did."

"Well, since someone hasn't called me and I was getting a bit worried, this was the only solution."

I snicker. "Ha. Ha. I'm sorry I haven't called. It's been so busy, and I am so tired."

"You know I'm just teasing. So it's going well?"

I hesitate. How much do I tell her over the phone? "It's wonderful here. Like being in revival."

"That's good. What's wrong?"

She never misses when I'm lying. "I'm worried about Adam."

"Is that all? Your kids are fine. Sound asleep." She laughs. "Okay not really. They are having a late movie night with my kids. All's well on the home front."

I chew on my lip. I need to talk to someone who won't judge me. And I can always count on Maggie. "It's not that. I saw a picture of Adam with his arm around some other woman. What if he is having another affair?"

"Oh, hon. You don't really think he would, do you?"

"I don't know."

"Want me to drive over there right now and see for myself?"

Sort of. "No. Of course not." I shake my head.

"I will. You know I will."

"Thank you. But no. I really just need to talk to him. It's been hard to get a hold of him with the time difference and all."

"There's no sense in worrying. Surely even a dumb man isn't dumb enough to do that to you twice."

"He's not dumb, Maggie."

"I know that." She huffs. "Listen, the best thing to do is pray. Want me to pray with you?"

"There's more."

"Oh?"

"Remember me telling you about the handsome man on the trip, Brant?"

"Yeah."

"He called me beautiful today. And I really liked hearing that."

"Of course you did. Who wouldn't?"

I'm going to wear a hole in my lip if I don't stop gnawing on it. "I almost did something really stupid." Tears spring to my eyes.

"Spill the beans. Now."

"I was really upset and I almost went to his room. I . . . I even went to his door."

"But you didn't. You stopped yourself."

"How do you know? You're not here."

"Because I know you. Listen." Her voice drops to her you'd-better-listen-to-me momma tone. "You are lonely. Not just because you've been over there alone. But because your marriage is struggling. Your husband doesn't treat you like he should. I bet Brant seems very caring and sensitive, doesn't he?"

"Yes."

"Have you considered the fact that he is hitting on a married woman?"

I squeeze my eyes shut. "No."

"What does that say about his moral character?"

"I don't know."

"It tells me he has no boundaries. He is reckless and over-confident. Is that really the type of man you would be attracted to?"

"No."

"You are vulnerable, Julie. And the devil is messing with your mind because you are out there doing a big thing for God. You had better not let him. You are better than this. Stronger than this."

I'm not. I am really not. But she has a good point. "I hadn't looked at it all that way before."

"I know. That's why I'm saying it now."

I giggle. "Gee, thanks."

"Sometimes we all need a little kick in the pants to see things for what they are. Now, seriously. Want me to go check on Adam?"

I really do, but I will not stoop to that level. "No. I'll call him this evening and set things straight."

"Good. Let's pray. Lord, please help Julie. She is feeling weak and scared, vulnerable to the devil's attacks. She is over there teaching Your babies about You, and we ask that you bind the devil, get him off her heart and mind, and cast him back into that lake of fire far away from her. Protect her heart from temptation. Protect her children from harm. And protect her husband from me."

A chortle escapes me. Leave it to Maggie to be able to make me laugh during prayer.

"Because if I find out he's hurt my best friend again, I'll whoop him myself. Amen."

"I love you, Mags."

"I love you too. Now get some rest and call me after you talk to Adam."

"I will."

"Promise?"

"Promise." I sigh, feeling the worries lifting and sleep hovering in the fringes of my mind. "Thank you. For everything. Kiss my babies for me, please."

"Already done."

I end the call and snuggle into the comforter. *Thank you for a friend who doesn't judge and who is always ready to be honest with me. Bless her, Lord.*

Knocking on my door jars me awake. Have I overslept again? I grab my phone and check the time. I've only been sleeping for thirty minutes. No wonder I feel so out of it. "Who is it?"

"It's Brant. I need to talk to you."

My stomach clenches. About what? "Okay. Just a minute." I climb from bed, straighten my clothes, and throw the covers over the pillows. When I crack open the door, he smiles.

"Sorry to wake you."

"Is something wrong?"

"Yes and no." He takes a step forward and pushes open the door, inviting himself into my room.

Come on in. I make sure to leave the door opened wide and turn to face him. "Okay. What's up?"

"I can't stop thinking about last night. I know you were at my door."

My eyes widen, and my pulse kicks into high gear. I open my mouth, but I can't think of a thing to say.

"You're unhappy. I can tell."

Still nothing coming from my mouth. My brain seems to have clogged.

"My wife suffered from serious depression after our daughter was born. She started drinking and eventually had an affair."

"I'm sorry to hear that." There, finally something coherent.

"Your husband has hurt you, hasn't he? I can see it in your eyes every time you mention him."

I nod slowly.

"I knew it."

He sounds so sure of himself. The words Maggie spoke earlier come spilling to the front of my thoughts.

"It was you at my door, wasn't it?"

His gaze is almost desperate somehow. As if he must prove himself correct. I don't want to answer him. But I can't lie either. "Yes."

He grins and rushes to stand in front of me. "I knew that too."

Of course he did. My heart is doing that stupid fluttering thing again, having him so near. I can smell his soap and the tangy scent of his deodorant. His minty breath.

This isn't right.

I take a few steps backward, pressing against the wall leading toward the doorway. "You should leave."

"Are you sure that's what you want?"

My body is protesting, but my heart is screaming above the noise. "Yes."

He drops his head but turns to me from the doorway. "I'm right next door if you change your mind."

I swallow. Hard. "No, Brant. I won't be changing my mind."

On shaking legs and with quivering everything, I shut the door behind him and slide to the floor. With my face buried in my hands, I allow myself to breathe for the first time since he knocked.

The nerve! How dare he assume what I want! How dare he take my unhappiness and tempt me to sin!

It's been a long time since I felt such violent heat scorching my veins. So much stronger than the piddly anger I felt at being left behind the other morning. No, this one is building up inside, lobbing emotional pinballs around my mind. I've half a mind to go to his door, and knock this time, so I can slap him good and hard. How could I have been so blind? Of course Maggie is right. Brant is willing to cross a line, the one drawing a line around my finger and my heart, making me off-limits, and not even feel badly about it. That is not a man I could ever be attracted to.

The fact that I have been ogling him for five days makes me want to smack myself. My stomach sours, and I rush to the bathroom. Splash cool water on my face, careful not to get any in my mouth or nose. No parasites, Philippines, please. I rinse the acidity from my mouth with bottled water and stare at my reflection. This is not how this trip was supposed to go. It was supposed to be God-centered, Scripture-focused, and Jesus-fixated.

This is my fault. Not Brant's. Not Adam's. And certainly not God's. How many times have I chastised my thoughts in the last ninety-six hours? More than I should have needed to. *Oh, I am so sorry, Lord.*

My alarm shatters the silence. It's time to get ready for evening service. Only a couple hours until I can set things right with Adam. Clear the air. Confess.

"And the LORD," Pastor Joel begins, "he it is that doth go before thee; he will be with thee, he will not fail thee, neither forsake thee: fear not, neither be dismayed."

My attention is riveted on him, even though one of my preschoolers has clambered into my lap and squirms relentlessly every few seconds. I've chosen a seat as far from Brant as possible, but I am still keenly aware of his presence. Though, the sweet girl in my lap keeps me grounded and the anger from dumping over.

"He is already where you are going. He is still where you've been. And he is exactly where you are in this moment. Don't you know how much God loves you? He is with you every step."

I draw a sharp breath to the chorus of loud amens. Yes, He is. That's right. He knows all about the battle I'm in, and I'm not fighting, not even for a second, alone. How can the devil win when God is on my side? He can't. Simple as that. This temptation will pass.

I squeeze my eyes closed and focus on which of my emotions are genuine.

The temptation has already passed.

My eyes fly open, the revelation springing joy within me. Brant's actions and Maggie's words have driven any attraction from my body and mind. Praise the Lord! In my head, I'm shouting.

I yawn as I dial home. Though my heart is pounding, the rest of me seems intent on sleeping only.

"Hey, hon." Adam's voice is surprisingly alert. I half-expected him to be sleeping in on Saturday morning while the kids ransacked the house.

"Hey. How's it going? Are the kids up?"

He chuckles. "Hold on, eager beaver. They are up, but don't I get to talk to you first?"

"I'm sorry. Of course. How are you?"

"You know me, regular ole super dad."

Right. I resist chortling and immediately scold myself. He is home alone with three kids while I'm gallivanting around the world. "You certainly are."

"How are you?"

Good. Bad. Homesick. A hypocrite. "I don't know."

"Tired?"

"Mm-hmmm."

"Hot?"

"Mm-hmmm."

He chuckles. "You're doing a good thing, Julie. Just remember that."

Oh, if he only knew where my thoughts had been. How do I tell him? With his voice happier than I've heard it in a long time and his desire to talk to me and his praises. I can't ruin it. Not now. "So, tell me about home. What's happening at church?" I hold my breath and pray it's good things.

"Well, it stormed like crazy when we were getting ready to leave Wednesday night. One of the ladies from the singles class broke her arm. She was freaking out about going out in the rain."

I swallow hard and try to avoid accusations. "Oh?"

"Yeah, I helped her get a rain coat on and took her to her car with an umbrella, just in case."

I hold my breath as the gears in my mind spin wildly. A raincoat and a broken arm? Was it truly that simple?

"Julie?"

"Sorry. I'm tired. That was very chivalrous of you."

"Nah, just saving my sense of smell. You know how bad those casts stink when they get wet. Remember Porter's?"

Laughter spills from me, relief sweeping out of my tight chest. "That was awful. Silly little guy. We warned him not to get in that puddle."

"You warned him."

Not a compliment, yet somehow I can tell that's what Adam is going for.

"I miss you, Julie."

I close my eyes for a moment and dive deep within the well of emotions I feel rising. He misses me. He is happy to be talking to me. His wife. Not some other woman. "I miss you too." And I do, for the first time in ages. I really miss my husband. All his annoying traits and dirty clothes piled next to the laundry hamper. And snoring and boring TV shows. "I'd better get to bed. I'm exhausted." I want to end the conversation on a good note, missing him, and sleep with the honeyed feeling that revelation has brought.

"Sleep well. I love you."

"I love you too."

Ending the call, I swipe open the Facebook app and look at the photo one more time. Sure enough, there is a bright pink raincoat in Adam's hand. And the tip of a bright pink cast peeking from its open front. A long sigh escapes my lips.

Thank You, Lord, for reminding me to get details before I reacted—well, out loud, anyway. Forgive me for jumping to conclusions in my mind.

It feels really good to miss Adam. I smile to my dark room and close my eyes. Sunrise is in six hours.

Chapter Fourteen

I need to pray.

The undeniable urge spurs me from my warm, surprisingly-fluffy-and-comfortable-for-less-than-ten-dollars-a-night bed.

Before I'm even fully awake, I find myself on my knees, forehead pressed to the cool tile. I have been wrong. I've boarded myself inside an impenetrable prison. Nailed the shutters tightly closed and padlocked the single point of entry. No one is allowed inside my fortress. It's where I keep my heart safe from further harm. Where I live inside a bubble of skepticism, allowing myself to deny hope in my husband. If I never allow my hopes to float—drown them in suffocatingly heavy iron—I won't be hurt.

Right.

That's working so well. I snicker at the irony as my runny nose and burst eyeballs make a puddle of my sorrow on the floor.

Lord, I'm so sorry. I haven't been the Godly wife you ask me to be. I've been overly critical. I've hurt Adam on purpose because I was hurting. I've created a pattern of worry that leads to mistrust and it is based on something he's repented for. And that I've supposedly forgiven him for.

Why? Why did Adam have to have an affair? Doesn't he see how it's made me crazy? Will it ever make a difference how much time has passed? Will I ever stop thinking about him with *her?*

I slide from my knees to rest prostrate on my stomach. Though words no longer form in my mind, my sobs are doing the talking. I can feel God demolishing the wall. With a few mighty strokes of His finger, erasing the years of bricks I've stacked. Named one by one and glued in with bitterness. Disappointment from missing Valentine's Day. Hurt from when he forgot to say my new haircut looked nice. The time he said our children are spoiled. Nightmares seeded in truth. Snide remarks. All of them printed like billboards on the ugly stones.

God could climb over. Could come sailing on the breeze over the barbed-topped walls. But have I truly let Him?

He shouldn't need an invitation to come through the door. And He should be present in there with me. No wonder it's been so lonely and dark. So cold and scary. I've been making Him perch on the edges. Wait at the fringes until I felt . . . what? He'd answered my prayers? He'd changed my husband? He'd fixed my life?

Lord, please forgive me! I mean it this time.

The satiny quiet of peace glides into my heart. Fulfilling, warm like a cup of tea on a sore throat. I didn't know I was missing it until this moment. In this empty hotel room a million miles from home. I've. Been. Wrong.

Me.

Not all Adam. Me. He is not perfect. But I'm far from it myself.

As the final tendrils of masonry around my heart come crashing down, I can breathe. Fully take a deep breath for the first time in years. And feel the tension ebbing away. Like the clear blue tide cleansing the white sand beach half a mile away.

It's almost as sweet as the day I accepted Jesus as my Savior.

Just as eye opening. Just as necessary.

Peace like a river fills my weary soul.

I slip back under the covers, every fiber of my body feeling strung with fresh hope, unburdened and lighter than

I've been in a very long time. Focused. The last few days I have left, I will not be distracted by the enemy's tricks. Though the sun hasn't yet risen, I feel new light around me. The walls are down! Flattened, crushed, their ashes blown away by my Father's sweet breath.

Today is going to be better than yesterday. Better than all the ones previous.

"*Mam* Julie!" The dark-eyed beauty that occupied my lap at last night's service is barreling toward me, her arms flung wide.

I scoop her into mine and squeeze, ever amazed that none of these littles seem to care one ounce about my sweaty neck. "I'm so happy to see you, Rosamie."

"*Magandang umaga, po.*"

"What does that mean?"

"Good morning, *po.*"

"Oh. Good morning to you too. Thank you for teaching me that."

Her eyes widen. "You want to learn more words?"

"I do." I really do.

She squirms to get out of my arms, and as soon as her feet land on the ground, she grabs my hand and pulls me toward the gazebo. "Get a paper, *Mam* Julie."

I giggle and tag along. "Yes, ma'am."

Next to her on the bench, I smile as she writes words and pronounces them slowly so I will understand, correcting me when my vowel sounds are out of place. What a lovely child! Intelligent, well-learned. I didn't expect that here.

I didn't expect a lot that happened here. Least of all what's happened to me.

I toss a glance Brant's direction. He lobs the volleyball over the net and pumps his fist. Prances around a bit and taunts the children on the other side. Has he always been so pompous? Probably. But I was blinded by . . . by what? His muscles? His face? More than likely, my own emotional angst. My own damaged heart searching for something it desperately seeks.

I need more from Adam. That's not wrong, is it? But I can see now that I do, in fact, want the more to come from him. That's a good thing. A really good thing.

"I can't believe it's our last day." Tears sparkle in the corners of Liza's eyes. "I will miss these guys."

I pat Rosamie's head. "Me too." There's no doubt that I will, but I'm so ready to go home. I miss my family. American food. American toilets. American safety. Never again will I take my country for granted. I've thought it a hundred times in the last week, but I really want to mean it. Really want to make it stick.

I already know when I return, this place will fade. These new convictions will fade. And my new contentment will dim. Life will return to chaos. Will I be able to hold on to this beauty? This wonderful revelation I've discovered? The old me is still here! I thought I'd lost her long ago. But she's still here, waiting for me to let her wake up.

Now that she's stirred, can I keep her conscious?

Lord, I hope so. Help me remember how I am right now, in this very moment. I've discovered what Philippians 4:12 means, how to make it actually work. Keep it forefront in my mind please, I beg you, Lord. Show me how to remain calm, forgiving, and patient with Adam. I know I've been grouchy and short tempered. Nagging and resentful. I release it all to You. I have faith that You will perform a miracle in us both.

"Breakfast is ready!" Anna yells from the doorway.

Our last delicious, Anna-cooked breakfast. I will look for Filipino recipes when I get home, especially pork and cabbage. How I've missed this wonderful genre of meals, I don't know, but now that I know about it I will be adding their flavor to my menu.

I sit with my plate, sandwiched between Liza and Lewis. I will miss so much about this place. The garden. The laughter. The fellowship.

Brant blesses our meal amid the chorus of children's shouts that drifts toward us. Life at home is too complicated. We have far too much. When I return, our focus will be on daily learning more about Him and His creation. Let the rest of the pieces fall where they may. We need more family time, filled with prayers and Bible studies. Games and giggles. And no electronics.

"Well, gang. Last day," Dot says. "We will have closing ceremony tonight and be on a bus headed for the airport at 5:00 AM sharp tomorrow."

I suppose it only makes sense that I'm torn about my feelings leaving, since I was so torn about them coming. If only I could take all these amazing new friends home with me and keep them in my pocket. The memories tucked in tight will have to do. Chances are I will never see them again.

Everything about this day has been bittersweet. The children's smiles and quick answers to my questions in class. The sweet, ocean-tinted breeze. The thought of leaving my Filipino family to return to mine. Everything.

Settling into one of the same types of plastic chairs I've occupied all week, I gaze slowly around me, taking in every detail. Lizard on the wall. Sparrow in the tree. Bat in the evening sky colored with shades of rose. I don't ever want to forget a single detail. But I know I will. Time always fades things for me.

Lewis takes the mic after another elaborate opening from Pastor Joel. Another thing I will miss. Who would've expected the people of this third-world country to be such wordsmiths? We have spent so much time expediting and efficiency-izing ourselves in the U.S., we've lost track of the simpler beauties in life.

Our last Philippines preaching seeps into my heart, gently, smoothly, without the terrible walls to climb over, bang against, disrupt before it can find its home. I take a deep breath, let it out slowly, and soak in the warmth of the word. *Please, Lord, no more walls.*

Chapter Fifteen

I am not going to cry. I am not going to cry. I swipe at the corner of my eyes as Anna releases me from a long hug. "I will miss you."

"I will miss you too. Thank you for coming to our little country."

What do I say? How can I explain to her how much her "little country" has changed me? I will never be the same. Never. "I . . . No, thank you. Really."

"You seem so," she touches my cheek, "happy today, *Mam* Julie."

"I am." But it's more than that. One word cannot explain it. I doubt I could explain it with a hundred.

All of our new friends line up to embrace us, to swipe at tears, and to thank us. It is almost more than I can bear. Saying goodbye and knowing thousands of miles will separate us for the rest of our lives. That in time names and faces will fade. But, hopefully, the seeds we helped plant in the children's minds will grow and mature and turn into fruit.

As we file out of the home church's front door into the star-blessed night, our friends follow in a bunch, waving and shouting blessings to our retreating backs. Into the group of trikes, onto the road toward the hotel for the last time. Passing the fields I've come to recognize, the *caraboa* I've secretly named. A final left turn into the parking lot. Tomorrow we will be on a plane for home.

Home.

That one simple word has never sounded so wonderful. I cannot wait to see my babies. To hold their warm, squirming bodies close and kiss their sweet-smelling heads. But the excitement that stirred me to restlessness on the trip here is not present. Replaced by a calm I can't remember ever feeling. *Thank you, Lord. For everything.*

"How can we have two sunsets in the same day?" Lewis wiggles his eyebrows and smiles.

I can barely hold my eyelids open. Thirty-plus hours of traveling and it is still the same date. My mind is much too tired to figure it all out. All I know is that the lights of Maryville are coming into view and my family is down there. Can't this plane go any faster?

We circle for what feels like hours, waiting for clearance, I guess. But it is torture. Onto the bumpy tarmac, the flight attendants remind us to grab our items. I don't even care if I remember everything. My family is waiting. My children are so close!

As I wait in line to exit the plane, I feel a tug at my elbow. Reluctantly I spin.

Brant smiles. "Are we good?"

I pause, trying to direct my thoughts away from my kiddos for a moment. "I don't really know what to say. I pray that you find what you need in this life."

"Same to you."

I allow the joy I feel to broaden my grin. "I already have, Brant."

If I could shove everyone aside and sprint out of the terminal, I would. My heart is beating a jittery rhythm. We round the corner and there, there in the corner stands my family. My handsome husband and three perfect babies. Tears spring to my eyes and rush down my cheeks. I drop my bags, fall to my knees, and scoop Eleanor, Porter, and Grace into my arms. Never have I felt such joy, such relief, such overwhelming love.

My knees are shaking as I release them and rise. Adam is staring at me, smiling with his head cocked to the left, holding a sign that says, Welcome home, Mommy. "Hi," he whispers.

"Hi." If my heart would stop pounding, maybe I could be a bit more eloquent. "I like the banner."

His chest puffs. "Thanks."

"I missed you."

He opens his arms and I rush into them, crushing the crinkly paper between us. He wraps them around me and squeezes. I sigh, relaxing into his strong chest. The man I fell in love with is back. I can tell by the softened lines framing his eyes. The kindness shining down at me.

He leans in and whispers, "Let's start over, Julie."

Chills rocket down my spine, tingling, exciting. "I'd love to."

About the Author

Sara is a multi-published, award-winning author and homeschooling mother of five who writes amid the beauty of East Tennessee. She earned her Bachelor's degree in Animal Science from the University of Tennessee and is a member of American Christian Fiction Writers. She is the author of the Love, Hope, and Faith Series, which includes *Callum's Compass* (2017), *Camp Hope* (2018), and *Rarity Mountain* (March 2019). She also has a story, "Leap of Faith," in *Chicken Soup for the Soul: Step Outside Your Comfort Zone*. Sara finds inspiration in her faith, her family, and the beauty of nature. When she isn't writing, you can find her reading, camping, and spending time outdoors with her family. To learn more about her and her work or to become a part of her email friend's group, please visit www.saralfoust.com.

Also by Sara L. Foust

Inspirational Romantic Suspense

Book #1 in the Love, Hope, and Faith Series

Kat Williams's brother died in a gruesome accident in the mountains of East Tennessee. She blames herself. Ryan Jenkins's fiancée was murdered. He couldn't protect her.

With the death of her brother, Kat believes she is unworthy of love from anyone—even God. When a good friend elicits a promise that she will stop living in the past, then leaves her clues to a real-life treasure hunt, Kat embarks on an adventure chock-full of danger. To find the treasure, Kat will have to survive wild animals—and even wilder men. Can she rely on Ryan, the handsome wildlife officer assigned to protect her ... without falling in love? Ryan swore off love when his fiancée was murdered, but feelings long buried rise to the surface around Kat. He volunteers to help with her treasure hunt, vowing to keep her safe. Together they venture deep into caves and tunnels ... and even deeper into the depths of their unplumbed hearts.

Available on Amazon now!

Book #2 in the Love, Hope, and Faith Series

AMY DAWSON directs a summer camp for foster children near Briceville, Tennessee. A foster mom for the first time, her responsibilities as mother to a traumatized child bring a whole new set of challenges and joys. But when Amy's four-year-old foster daughter is dragged into the mountains of Royal Blue by a former employee, parenting challenges are overshadowed by a new nightmare. The Sheriff's department fails to procure viable leads, and Amy can't sit idle. Her childhood friend and first love, JACK EVANS, returns to lend his skills as tracker. Problem is, he also stirs up romantic memories Amy would rather leave buried.

Jack struggles to let go of his past failures and prove his reliability by bringing Mattie home, but fears when he left camp fifteen years ago and failed to keep a promise to Amy he permanently lost her confidence.

As Amy plunges into the wilderness on horseback to search for Mattie, she must decide who she trusts, let go of her childhood traumas, and learn to rely on hope in God. Facing dehydration, starvation, and a convoluted kidnapper, will she succeed in recovering her precious foster daughter or get lost in the vast wilderness forever?

Available on Amazon, Books A Million, and Barnes & Noble now!

Book #3 in the Love, Hope, and Faith Series

Rarity Mountain-Coming March 2019!

On the surface, SIMON FINCUFF and FERN STRONGBOW have nothing in common. Simon has served his sentence, but his past conviction still haunts him. Fern is a veterinarian and grew up on an off-the-grid homestead. The one thing they share? Each has a dark secret they would do almost anything to protect.

When their current careers are yanked away, they are left scrambling to pick up the pieces. A reality television show falls into their paths, offering a life-changing opportunity that tests their resolve and their faith.

These two unlikely partners must battle to survive for thirty days in the untouched wilderness of Rarity Mountain with only a handful of survival items and a director who is out for drama, no matter the cost. With their lives and their carefully guarded skeletons on the line, they will discover how far they are willing to go to win the million-dollar prize for Survival Tennessee.